Jacob White

Being DEAD in SOUTH CAROLINA

stories

Leapfrog Press
Fredonia, New York

Being Dead in South Carolina© 2013 by Jacob White

Published in 2013 in the United States by
Leapfrog Press LLC
PO Box 505
Fredonia, NY 14063
www.leapfrogpress.com

Printed in the United States of America

Distributed in the United States by
Consortium Book Sales and Distribution
St. Paul, Minnesota 55114
www.cbsd.com

First Edition

Author photo courtesy of Kevin Dossinger

ISBN: 978-1-935248-44-6

Library of Congress Cataloging-in-Publication Data

Available from the Library of Congress

for Somer

Contents

Being Dead in South Carolina

Look. Have you ever tried to right a car you yourself have tumbled? I mean, working alongside a few others, rocking the dumb hulk back and forth in hopes of landing it back upon its four sound tires? No, of course not. You have no idea. This is one of those thousand lucky adventures (mark I said *lucky*) that one's idea of life never allows for. Or if it does happen, your memory won't know what do with it, with the strange articulation of stupidity and rebirth that is an overturned car. It's the sort of story you expect to tell your asshole friends years later but never do, never do because you don't know what else will come spilling out.

I'll say this. Standing there on that road bank, kneading ditch-side clay with your silly feet and trying to look away from what you've just done—crows cawing overhead—where you've been and where you're going fall away, and you might as well be standing on some strangely dry and palpable beach, tossed there suddenly after murky years of sea change. You hear the faraway suck of tide. Your legs quiver like a doe's. But it's not you. It's me. Me on an elbow of county road somewhere in Chester, me standing here, looking at a rolled car. Me, some others, pushing at this car. Trying to right it.

Jacob White

I'm with my Uncle Russ and my cousin Jackie, whose Chevelle I have afflicted. I haven't visited them since I was ten, when Russ used to torque out the scooters Jackie and me raced meanly around their farm house. This was before Russ moved his family down to Chester and Jackie grew up to be a testy little shine-headed son of a bitch foreman. A Christian, on top. A Methodist Christian, on top. Russ, he looks a bit soggier than he did twenty years back, but he's still in charge. I had to beg Jackie to drive the car. Beg.

Chester's an hour south of York, where I was born and still live. These Chester crows sound different than York ones. Older. Parched. I hardly know these people next to me, pushing at this car.

Why I am here with these grayer and more humorless versions of my childhood friends is by order of my mother, so I can reassociate my memory, which is defective somewhat. Or so say the doctors, ever since a bullet passed through my head last April and hit, it turns out, very little. I try telling Mother my memory feels fine, but she shakes her finger at my forehead and says, "We got to reassociate it, Dayton." Plus she thinks Jackie's going to turn my life around. She thinks Jackie the Methodist foreman can talk to me about the long range. "If we're going to fix that head, we got to yank it from your ass, boy." I've long suffered from shortsightedness, she says. And bad judgment as a result.

And it goes to show you, because what I am thinking of as I grunt up against the car's wide-hipped hull is not what a whoop-dee-doo adventure life is but how my cousin Jackie has just punched me in the mouth, which is what you do with some no-account cousin who's just rolled the Chevelle you've been restoring for eight years. Like a no-account, I am fretting over a loose tooth as I push and so only half pushing.

10

Being Dead in South Carolina

Now imagine among us, too, as we begin to rock this car toward rectitude, a woman. (Here, the lucky part.) She is, like us, asquat, grunting, rippling with a confusion of muscle and gristle. A strand of hair sticks to her plump cheek; hamstrings quiver through the dimpled backs of her legs; "Uhn-nf," she says, "shit." She was at their house this morning when I showed up with my duffel. Jackie'd met her at church and introduced her as Peat—"spelled like the moss," said Jackie, and he can't even say *this* without it sounding high and mighty. It irritates the hell out of me. It irritates me more that my cousin who I always made fun of for being ugly is engaged to a real live beautiful woman. Anyway, it's me, Jackie, Russ (who does nothing about the punching business, just stands and watches me take it—*knowing* I'd take it), Peat as in the moss, and then the gnarled black guts of this car, steam hissing up as if to draw out the word *consequence*. I've been in Chester maybe an hour.

So here's me one night six months ago. I'm carrying two bags of groceries out of Harris Teeter when out in the parking lot this dark voice is at my back. "Paper or plastic, dribble-dick?" he says, then shoots me in the head to let me know he's being rhetorical. It was shortly before this parking lot business my wife and son left; and shortly before they left that I'd shown up at the house after a three-dayer and tried to recruit my son Elden for a road adventure. I shook him from his pillow: "We're going on a road tear, boy. West and all." His hair's curly as hell. He bore back under the covers and I shouted at him fine then, that I'd go find me a raven-haired Indian boy out west who'd count for crud when it came to first-basing and showing respect. Which is about when Trudy showed up, collared me into the hall as if to talk, and then—as I hung

11

my head and exhaled and waited for her to start in—maced me. I screamed in a way that might emphasize the severity of what she'd just done. But she didn't even call the cops. Just kicked at my shanks until I was outside again, windmilling down the middle of our street hollering, "Shakespeare don't know! Shakespeare don't even *know*!" I stayed at my mother's a week until Trudy and Elden cleared out, then went back to the house and chose as the first of many dismal tasks to restock the fridge. Trudy usually shopped at BiLo, but even though Harris Teeter costs more, it's a great place to get your morale back.

So you can see why, waking up in that hospital room, I was sure I'd done all this to myself. That I'd pulled the trigger. I was a bit shocked by my resolve. Then I was a bit proud. Picture me there, in that glowing moment just before I'd fully awoken to these last six months of afterlife: feeling at my crooked crown of bandages, semi-inclined and grinning; in my head bustling, already, the drama of Trudy and Elden crowding my bed saying *why, why*, humbled and mightily impressed by my solemn act. Me saying into a hand-mirror, "Dayton, you done it now, boy."

But it turns out I didn't think this idea up. The world thought it up for me. My friend Diamond managed to think it up for himself a few years ago. His first try hadn't come off: his wife came home early one night with Chinese and found him standing in the shower with his electric guitar, it plugged in to an amp on the toilet lid. Lukewarm water spattered over him as he strummed some mess. "What was he playing?" some smart guy once asked her. But there was only a soggy flub-flub sound, articulation not being the point.

What Diamond ended up articulating to himself was a hollow-point from his daddy's Ruger. This was a year later.

Being Dead in South Carolina

But all anyone ever thinks of anymore is him standing in that shower, naked, strumming and, more likely than not, singing, moaning through verses of lyrics he'd never known. (I say why bother getting naked if you're going to finish yourself off in the shower playing an electric guitar—your statement will just get confused.)

Anyway, learning from some clever decatheterizer that I was shot not by my self but by Mr. Voice (who my dreams would reintroduce me to, eventually) has been one of the greater disappointments of my life.

The bullet went in behind the ear and sort of fell out of my temple.

That I can walk and talk and still hit the toilet makes me something of a miracle in the medical community. My memory has gone spotty—I'm sure whole years are missing—but I don't notice. The thing is, I can't remember if I ever remembered those years to begin with. I wish Trudy and Elden were here. Trudy would let Elden and me sit up late with her in the kitchen as she played her Townes Van Zandt tapes, telling us, *Listen, this one's about heartbreak,* or *This one's about pickup-truck love.* Now they are some place I can't find them. They know nothing of how I was victimized in a parking lot. "We are going to have to write you off, Dayton," the letter said. In cursive! If only she could see me, lying in a mess of blood and instant mashed-potato flakes (the canister went off like a roman candle when I fell on it). It might help if Trudy were here to tell me about some of those small, gem-like moments as she used to call them, precious little flickers of memory from the tinkerbox of her mind which whenever she brought them up I'd pretend to remember too. Some summer night we sat out in the truck and talked till dawn, or one of our trips to Myrtle Beach which was more special than the others, a nap we took in a canoe out on Lake Jocassee, the birds there . . .

Nowadays I spend my afternoons at Mother's. I lie on the couch and try to keep breathing as she digs through my old toy chest and hoists up skates and pistols and stuffed chipmunks which maybe she expects me to bat around like a half-wit. She keeps saying, "I know you remember *this*" before pulling the artifact out, and after about every three *Remember this*es I cover my face and say, "Uhg—burn it, Mother!" From the hallway her boxy clock ticks away stale afternoon hours. "As-so-ci-ate! As-so-ci-ate!" she cheerleads, using a monkey and tow truck as pom-poms. No thank you.

Like I said, the weekend at cousin Jackie's was her idea. On top of edification, she said it's the happiest she ever saw me, when I was ten and tearing around the house on those scooters with Jackie. But who *isn't* happy then? Dazed and muddy-kneed, too nearsighted to know you're just doing circles. I ask: Who *isn't*?

There are things I remember now I'm not sure I remembered before. Like the day I winged Jackie with a .22. He was setting up Sun Drop cans. It's like me to forget we weren't using pellet guns anymore (by ten, both our backs were thoroughly pocked from those pump rifles). Anyway, he howled and ran at me holding his shoulder like someone named Igor. Ran at me the same way you run at the no-account cousin who has just rolled your just-waxed hotrod—yelling back then just like he did today, soon as everyone'd crawled out the Chevelle windows and scrabbled up from the dust—"I'll kill you!" Jackie's was a rage you get only when someone does exactly what you expect them to do. His face wadded into a rag of disgust—a countenance, I'm afraid, that plagues the

Being Dead in South Carolina

faces of all my kin in their moments of fixing or scrubbing or sleeping.

The bullet went clean through Jackie that day—we never found it—and I know Jackie's preaching to himself how the bullet that got me was the same. Like while I've been living a slacker sort of existence all these years—pawing after women, reeling out of bars, denting up friends' cars, occasionally chopping trim at the door mill—that bullet's been crossing oceans and continents, headed right for me. For the back of my head. It sounds a mean thing to think, but you don't know Jackie. His is a strange brand of Christianity. For all I know, he spent his youth matriculating his way toward Adult Sunday School. Now he's a big shot on the site and what he tells my mother after Trudy and Elden left is that I *just wasn't ready.* He's got a mousetrap for a heart.

Anyway, the day I shot Jackie, Russ had to take the .22s away and lock them up until next summer. Uncle Russ is an old-time carpenter and the type who says nothing except for the very pinnacle of what is obvious and true, but says it in a way that puts the world more in square, knocking you like a nailhead flush with the truth of life, and what he said that day, laying his soft blue eyes on me, was, "Son, you ruin about everything." I don't remember remembering this before, but I remember it now. Uncle Russ is all right.

After half an hour or so pushing against the discouraging weight of that car, we finally get it over. It's dented up pretty much all round, roof scalped of paint. The back windshield is cracked. First thing, Jackie runs around and leans in the driver's window to see if it'll start, and it does. We pile in, Peat and I in back. All I need is a dunce cap. Since the struts are jammed, Jackie surrenders the wheel to Russ, who, shifting into drive, right away produces one of his small miracles of sound judgment by announcing, "Well, let's try to get her to Gibson's." Gibson's being Chester's version of a bar and where I suspect Russ continues his tradition of ordering a mug of beer and not drinking it. The one time I ever saw my uncle take a drink was after I shot Jackie. He pulled a Schlitz from under the workbench in his garage, cracked it, took a sip, and leaned there for an hour staring out at god knows what.

In front of me, Jackie, who never graduated from Sun Drop, hangs his head out the window, inspecting the dangle of fender, the warp and splay of tires. He's fat now but still moves with the fitful jerks of a wound-up six-year-old—he's about to bust the seat back. It annoys me enough to make me forget this is all my fault. I look out the window and shake my head, working at the tooth with my tongue. I can feel my lip swelling. After a while I spit the tooth into my palm. It's from somewhere in the incisor region. In my hand it looks small and ugly as hell, a sliver. I see Peat's watching, and I flash her my new smile. Jackie's handiwork has left me with the grin of a fifth-grade bully.

"That lip'll turn plum black," she says.

"Someone's got to do the Lord's work," I say.

"Hurt?"

"Not much."

"Not much," she repeats.

"Yeah."

"I'll bet."

The afternoon is getting late. We pass a gas station and its light swims across those knees of hers—they're drawn up against the vinyl back of Russ's seat, looking both sexy and fulsomely generous. She's got those heavy round legs I have often looked to for salvation. I think of her putting her back

Being Dead in South Carolina

into that Chevelle, her crosstrainers sliding in the mud. The smell of her black hair makes my leg tremble. I want to steal her from Jackie. Me with my fifth grader's smile. Add to this the little dollop of scar tissue behind my ear—it could pass for a cigarette burn. It's worse at my temple, where the bullet nudged its reluctant exit, but I comb over it.

At one point she looks over and says, inexplicably, "Jackie thinks you might should come live with him and Russ. For a while. Jackie can put you to work."

Suddenly it's too small in the car. I wriggle my knees, a little rough on the back of Jackie's seat, which he won't move up (he's still hanging out the window, hollering something to Russ, who's trying to steer). "No offense," I say, going for some high and mighty of my own. "But Jackie don't *get* it." We sit there for a minute. "Besides," I say, "I'm pretty swamped"—I flick my head back toward York.

When I'm not at Mother's, I sit out in my front yard in a plastic Adirondack, staring not at the highway but at my own house, my memory working hard to fill it up.

"Well," she says, "fine. We didn't know you were so busy," and I think she's going to drop it. Then, "Someone tries to help you and you get all prickly about it."

"I need help now? That what this is? I am your Christian brother and whatnot?"

"For now I'd say more along the lines of whatnot."

This shuts me up for a minute. "What kind of Christian are you, anyway?"

"The kind not afraid to split your other lip."

I think about this for a while.

Gibson's is crowded and people are even dancing. It's mostly old couples. South Carolina's turned into all old people recently. I follow them over to a lacquer-encased booth. All three slide in one booth seat. I sit in the other. They look at me.

"Mercy," Russ says, knocking up the brim of his boxy Firestone cap an inch, signifying to us that our ordeals are over and it's now time to ponder what bigger picture there is. Which I'm doing okay at when a waitress comes by, looks at me, and says to the rest, "That whuppin he taked still *workin* on him." This is Chester for you.

"I taked worse," I say as she skirts off.

Russ chuckles, then pulls his brim back down, leaning forward. "Dayton, son, you're a damn mess. Stay on a while. Jackie'll keep you busy at the site. Right, Jackie?" He leans back, the matter settled.

"Don't bother," says Peat. "He's swamped."

"Oh? That so, son?" says Russ, perking up—believing it, bless him.

"Well . . ." I give a *little of this, little of that* shrug.

Jackie eats peanuts shell and all, glancing at me like what I say and don't say from here on out is as predetermined as dog coil.

"He can't hardly get *away*," Peat says.

It's not her fault, but this is a tender subject. I recovered months ago, but Mallard Doors never gave me a formal invite back to the mill, where I ran the trim saw for almost a year. For eight months. Turns out I didn't show up to work much. Anyway, I got to housepainting with my high school friend Grady up till a week ago, when I saw he never intended to pay me. Packing my duffel in York this morning, I was part contemplating my empty house and part contemplating how on Monday I'd have to show up by Grady's truck after work with a mattock handle or some kind of other handle. How

Being Dead in South Carolina

I'd say, You know what, I got to eat too, bud. I've been thinking on this all weekend, on how to hit him in the head just
right so that he'll feel some pain before he goes soft and lies
down. My life's always dumping me into this sort of dilemma.
I swear to god it's easier for some people.

"Look at him," Jackie says, who I'm getting tired of already. "He don't got a job. Look at him."

I think of Jackie hitting me. How I felt the bottom half of
my face smear away for a moment, then eyed him right back.
Eyed him and did nothing.

I slide back out of the booth, saying I'd like to buy the
table a round—a gesture I hope will wipe the know-it-all
satisfaction off everyone's face.

I'm standing at the bar, and this cowboy type sitting next
to me looks up and says, "Fella, looks like you got some jam
there on your lip." I look down at him. I can't tell if he's being
smart or not. "And looks like you got a mouth full of shit,
bud," I say. The guy's handsome smile kind of hangs there; he
keeps his eyes on me. The beer arrives.

When I get back to the table they're already talking
amongst themselves. I fill their glasses as they talk about some
good body man named Clive, about what parts need ordering
and from where, about repair and the clear steps toward it.
No one expects me to help. I'm pouring my second before
I notice the others haven't touched theirs. I stare off. I study
the measly, retriever-sized head of a black bear and, as my
beer dwindles, begin to deem it the saddest species on earth.
It looks almost apologetic. Its mouth is open with the *I* in
I'm sorry.

Then Russ pops his elbow onto the lacquered tabletop.
His old fry-pan palm up in the air. "Let's get it one time, son."
It takes me a minute to decipher through the heavy squint of

his old age that merry look which he used to give me in my scooter years whenever I shouldered in through the screen-door looking mean or upset. We'd arm wrestle and he never once let me win.

Lately I am working on being a good sport. I grind my elbow into the salt grit, take hold. "All right, Russ." I cock my eyebrow.

Jackie's eyes fret across the table like insects, for once not knowing what'll happen next.

"Give you a chance to whup up on somebody," Russ says. "Easy now," he says, but the way his big hand chokes down on my own suggests he's talking more to himself.

Last week I woke up on the garage floor with Elden's old Schwinn on top of me. I was holding it to my chest like a blanket. Inside, my machine winked with that terrifying red light. I pushed it and out poured some bad-breathed racket: a barroom, someone yelling at me—"Are you there? Are you there, Dayton?"—only it was my own voice, jagged and top-heavy, trying to out-yell the crybaby inside of me.

Old Russ's getting me, growling into me. He can't help but be excited because he's getting me. He feels how all my tautness has gone out, how something inside me has unstrung, come loose. And I catch that fellow at the bar pointing me out to three other fellows and having a chuckle. I look at him as if to say, "What's so funny, dribble-dick?" He looks at me with some kind of narrow brown eyes, then looks away—like he's seen right through to what I am and that what I am is common manure. I keep staring at him, hard. I want him to know he can't pull that snicker and turn away shit with me. Like he's some Townes Van Zandt or something. Don't pull that flinty-eyed shit with me.

When I look back in front of me Russ's eyebrows are

flapping up and down like crazy and his mouth has got this twisted gape like he's trying to sing in French. I got his arm pressed to the table; his fingers are open under my fist, gnarled and writhing. "Oooh-oooh-gahh!"

"Hey, boy!" Jackie says. He goes to snatch my arm away, but I let go, hold my arms up. I'm sort of grinning. Peat shakes her head.

Russ takes off his Firestone hat, wipes his brow. His temples pulse a bright pink. He's panting. "I guess you did need someone to whup up on." He looks down at his opening and closing hand. A clear, sober drop of sweat comes off his nose.

"No dang sense of *humor*," Jackie spits at me and sits back down. I don't get it.

"Well," I say at him, "I guess the look on your face is pretty goddamn funny."

My missing-tooth smile absolves me, somehow. But all three of them are looking back at me funny—Jackie not even like he wants to kill me. They're looking at my temple, I realize; my hair has fallen into my eyes. I sweep it back over the red sunburst of flesh.

Rubbing his wrist, Russ says, "I guess you think you ought to died."

I shrug, trying to smile still. I pretend it's a good question.

Peat orders a round of Cokes. The scar bothers her, I see. Or maybe she's just bored; maybe she's thinking what is she doing with me and the hillbillies when there's Townes Van Zandt over there.

"Dying don't make people forget what sort of man you are," Russ says.

Jackie does his annoying drop-and-hook nod, like a nod and a shake at the same time, and says like they've had this conversation before, "The dead don't tend to improve."

I spread my arms, I hold tight to my grin. "I look dead to any of you?"

Russ glances at Peat, like to apologize for me having said whatever I might've said to her, and then looks at me and says, "You look tired, son."

Mornings lately I wake up panting, my vision bursting with sharp light and flickers of snake tongue, the world pulsating with the blue and red of vein work. Out my window I see peacoated backs hunching behind trees. I worry about the police, and about a blacker tide. Other mornings I just lie there and think how the world is too heavy with machinery. Sometimes I lie there for hours. No shit I look tired.

A song ends. The dance floor settles. Pool balls crack somewhere.

"No matter," I say, a new song strumming into the air. "I'm heading out West anyway. I'm made for desert living, I can tell."

Their gazes dangle over the table. Even Peat's.

Then Peat laughs—it just sort of spills out. The others chuckle in, too. And I can't help but get tickled, and then we're all laughing hard, even Jackie. He's laughing so hard he's all gums. Like when we were kids and I had over-wheeled or something. His whole bald head the meanest pink you ever saw, trembling to blow—and Peat laughing so hard at *that*. I'm laughing a long minute or two after they've stopped. Soon we're sipping our Cokes, exchanging stories of the ridiculous. Peat describes the likes of Jackie in his white choir robe, and I can see him fidgeting up there, his little pink head rotating this way and that. Jackie tries to embarrass Russ with an old one about the time he dynamited a stump through a neighbor's house. Russ tells one about Peat:

"She's over on that barstool there, eighteen years old, and

this boy, he comes up like he wants to tell her a secret, which she seems all for it until he gets to flicking this pink tongue in her ear. I'm sitting right here, and I get up—you know I can't stand this kind of shit. But same time, this one here, she slides off her stool, rocks back on one boot heel—you could hear the floorboard creak—and packs him in the forehead hard enough to unhinge a barn door." He slaps his knuckles into his fry-pan palm, then his hand into the table to show how the fellow went down. It cracks us up.

It's my turn for a story. And stories are one thing I have hundreds of. They look at me, faces slack with residual grins. But suddenly I'm tired of all my stories. I look at Peat. "I want to dance with you," I say in front of them. And for some reason she nods; for some reason she gives me her hand and, without a look to either of them, leads me through the tables before Jackie can notice, his chortle trailing off behind us—"Hard enough to kill a hog . . ."

I am now trying to hold the world responsible for some sort of articulation. Or else you slide loose and end up upside down in a ditch. Or you're calling yourself from a payphone. You're written off, is what you are—written off in *cursive*. It's about when you figure out the rest of the world has been listening to songs for the lyrics, and there you are in the shower with a guitar, trying to play the mush you were listening to when you should've been listening to the words—it's about then that you start to listen up.

My hand worries stiffly over the fleshy ravine in the small of her back; hers, miraculously, hangs over the back of my shoulder. The warmth I've been feeling among these people all day hits me. Whatever the song is, I love it.

I say, not too close to her ear, "This man is telling about

heartbreak, if you listen." I've never been much for music before.

"That's what all men are telling about." We've struck a nice rhythm, a careful sway.

"It's a particular one, Peat."

"Particular heart? Or you mean break?" She's making fun of me.

"Don't ruin it."

And whatever this is, it's not ruined. We work a tight circle under drunken sprays of light.

I'm digging up more of these gem-like moments lately. For instance: we *did* get that Chevelle over, after all. We somehow got it up to a point for gravity to take over. There was no groan, no crackle of glass as we let go, just a metallic creak of the sort that runs through your grandpa's recliner Sunday afternoons. The car towered for a moment up on its side, images of sky and tree slipping across the windshield—then it fell onto its tires and sat there, a bit brow-bent. You imagine a thunderous noise but there was none. Imagination's got nothing to do with it. The world sometimes has to imagine things up for you.

Less important is how the struts got jammed up; how Uncle Russ had to steer the ruined car to Gibson's through some drunken counterclockwise cursive. Or how things didn't go so hot with my wife and son. It's less important, for now. It's got to be. That's what some dumb miracle like getting a car turned back over is good for—blinding you to what came before it. To what comes after.

Which all I'm aware of tonight, even as we dance. For now, I hold as tightly to her as to the present. We are dancing. We dance. And later, when I'm outside giving it to Townes Van

Being Dead in South Carolina

Zandt on the gravel, seeing out of the corner of my eye Peat hurrying Russ into the busted car and Jackie getting rough-armed back by the clientele, I know I'm tearing once again from the cradle of kindness. I've been born again a thousand times, and each time's scarier than the last. You know what I mean? No, of course not. And that's the hell of it. It's about when Townes goes down, head clicking off a hubcap, and some others are on me, knocking teeth out of my head, air out of my lungs, sight out of my eyes, that the voice I hear in the dark becomes my own, saying as I fall backward, "Who's behind me? Who's behind me?"

Bethel

It was lying in bed at night I used to think of him. I'd click off the lamp, let a *Conan* flap to the floor, then pull that sad old quilt over me. I listened to a wide locusty static settle over the pasture. Gradually my eyes got accustomed to the dark, and I could make out the quilt's patchwork stretched before me—crop fields glimpsed from a mountain pass. I thought of great distances and what it meant to travel them. And that's when I could see him, my brother, appearing over some snowy curvature of earth, a man now—bearded, I was sure, shrouded in bear hide, our old hound Skokey ranging off a ways.

I was twelve; I had never left northern Missouri. Seeing the wider world in a patchwork quilt was possible for me then. Corey'd been gone six years, half my life, long enough to become a giant—the world itself nearly. I forgot all about what a son of a bitch he'd been as a kid, how he'd quarter a barn cat or open hand Mother or twist my arm harder than you ought a boy my age. Mother blamed it on he was a blue baby—came out in a noose. He was troubled. But the day he left I forgot all that stuff, remembering only the mythic circumstances of his departure. The papers had called him a killer and the papers were right. He'd busted free of something,

everything, and now he was somewhere I couldn't imagine—
ripping through man and beast, whipping at a world finally
big enough to take it. "Out there getting the poison out,"
Mother said often those six years he was gone, folding some
shirt of his she'd come across.

Still now, thirty-five years later, it's that slim hour before
sleep I think of after I click off my rig's fuzzy radio, two hundred night miles ahead of me. It's that faded quilt, glorious
gory Conan, and somehow my brother, the visions I had of
him, how all this together could lift me beyond the outlines
of my childhood. Looking back, of course, my childhood was
still firmly upon me, and it now seems inevitable that on one
particular night as I lay there dreaming of his bone heavy
footfalls, his wide winter breaths, the winterkill lolling across
his shoulders, I should hear the floor give some, and see beyond the flat fields of my quilt the full shadow of my brother,
standing at the foot of my bed, his back to me as he unbut-
toned a flannel shirt.

• • •

He'd run off plenty as a kid. Weekly, gone days at a time. But
the night he left us for good I remember. I was six, Corey
sixteen. He sat on the edge of his bed in his garage dungarees and hunting boots, stuffing a duffel with uncharacteristic
forethought. Jeans, BVDs, deodorant, a comb. His face held a
strange ash in the lamplight. A brown crust flecked his knuckles and forearms. "Go back asleep, Pickle." He said it firm,
not mean. I closed my eyes; I slept. Only later was I waked
by the hallway ruckus that always attended his departures—
the sinewy, red hot curses; bodies hitting walls; my brother's
voice breaking into a womanish yowl; Mother calling, "Careful, Paul!" The bedroom door bowed in; the handle jiggled.

Pop could often corral Corey back into our room, but I'd locked it when the fighting started and lay curled up under my covers. Finally the downstairs door slammed. The house went quiet. Then Mother let loose a long gut-sob I'd never heard before.

He'd been gone a day when word came of a man turned up dead over in Emden. The man was a forty-eight-year-old ex-con who'd come on as a tire-buster at the garage where Corey helped out. Corey got under a car himself now and then but mostly just helped out. The owner knew Pop. Not long after the ex-con started on, another guy there was killed when a car came off its jacks. I expect Corey saw it, saw it wasn't an accident like everyone said. Months later, up in Emden one February morning, a neighbor noticed the ex-con's front door half open, a socked foot hanging out. "Face all stove in," I remember an older kid on the bus saying. Buried in that face was a ball-peen hammer, Corey's, a recent birthday gift from Pop. Pop identified it for the police. It's funny, I can't anymore recall the Emden fellow's name. Big son of a bitch, I'd heard.

Both our nattered birders had tried to leave with Corey. But the next day, just after Pop saw off the two Emden cruisers and was walking back to where I sat on the porch step—holding out to me a G. I. Joe doll he'd found in the drive—Sister came tearing down our dirt road. We could see her pinned-back ears over the highgrass. Pop's hand sank back to his side, still dangling the doll by its boot as we watched. We both climbed up on the edge of the porch and craned as Sister rounded down a hard wheel rut of our drive, looking smaller now that for once Skokey wasn't with her. The dog leapt up on the porch and heeled with her chest pressed against Pop's leg, panting, glancing wildly around her. Only then did Pop's gaze falter from the road bend she'd come around.

Pop'd come up on a dairy farm and tried it himself, but after having me he had to turn to something more profitable and went into hardware. The store forever teetered on the brink, and at the end of a long day puttering with displays and scribbling in his ledger Pop came home looking not so much tired as strained, scuttle-eyed, his voice gone petty. Always in the breast of his coveralls was a small wire rust brush frayed to the wood.

Corey could always pull some red into Pop's cheeks, and while I'm sure Pop was some relieved to see my brother take his furies into the wider world, not having Corey there to fight against every day made him appear instantly old, standing there on that porch. In the weakening light his once jowly face seemed to sink and gray like weathered wood. Soon I'd begin to realize, at too young an age, that my father was just a man who wanted always to complain but never did because he knew he oughtn't.

Pop turned back toward the porch shade, toed Sister out of the way, and walked inside. I was surprised later to find the doll grimacing up from my grip.

Lowering his heft onto the other twin, a small blue flicker glanced from Corey's eyes: he knew I was awake.

"Pickle," he said, lying back and exhaling. The cherrywood frame popped and cracked under him. It suddenly felt natural to me he was there.

"Skoke outside?" I said.

He breathed. "Skokey. He got off in some woods. Up in"—he yawned—"up in Dakota. I'm going to sleep now, Pickle."

"All right."

He rolled onto his side and coughed, curling in his shoulders atop the quilt like some nomad.

"Bet you're tall now," he yawned, and we let off at that so sleep could bring him the rest of the way home.

Next morning, a bitter rot scorched the air in my room. His quilt was creased rather than rumpled, flattened with a stale sleep. I opened a window.

From downstairs came the warble of dishes hitting the table; bacon was frying, and Mother was already in her hardshoes, crossing and recrossing the receding linoleum. I put on a red snap front and tucked it into my jeans, looked in the mirror, then took it off. I cuffed the sleeves of a tee shirt and headed down.

"Why, that ain't *my* boy," Mother said cheerily. "Not no more." She wiped her knuckles with a dishrag and gestured out the window. "Out there chopping since *six*."

"Where's Pop?"

"Out with him. Tell them breakfast is on."

Out in the yard Corey was just lifting into his backswing, his figure arcing tall, his hind foot about to bust through the side of a water-rotted sneaker. His back was to me. He wore the red plaid flannel and jeans he must have arrived in—I never saw a duffel. Hair hung over his ears, oily and darker than I remembered. He did have a beard—mostly scraggle, wiry black half circles: a boy's beard. The part of his jowls I could see didn't look boyish at all, though—rubbery and pocked, swollen with the long-sickened, gray-meat pallor I've since grown used to seeing on hitchers.

It was about here I forgot about the bear hide nonsense, and not long after till I left off *Conan* altogether.

Bethel

The screen door clapped behind me. He glanced back—"Pickle"—then broke the quiet suspension of his arc with a jerky, violent swing whose impact was murderous and effective, sinking in with a sad *thunk* and setting his greased hair atremble. White splinters shot out and slowed against the air; cloven wood clinked onto more wood.

Just outside the circle of kindling stood my father. A white tuft lifted from his scalp in the breeze. He was squinting in the morning light and smiling.

He'd grown big, my brother. But it was a sunken weight. A carried weight. He bent for another log of pine, grunting, the flannel pulled tight across the meaty bunch of belly and breast. Standing back up, palming the nine-inch diameter of a log, he faced me for the first time, half grimacing, half smiling, his eyes closer set than I remembered.

Over breakfast, my folks didn't ask what he'd been doing or where because it would've come out as reproof. In talking to us Pop had always to restrain the reproof from his voice, never understanding that it was the restraint more than the reproof that set Corey off most. Pop held back with me too, but differently. Like I was too tender for his judgment. Or, more likely, like I was never really his to judge. I was called a sweet boy. Pop and I never fought much, not like he did with Corey. Lying in bed once, I heard him and Mother talking low on the porch. They were talking about something, not me, but my name came up and Pop sort of let off a minute. Then he uttered something in which I made out the word "drifty."

"Ducie, we got ten winters of wood out there!" Pop said now, leaning back his chair. His eyes were wide and slapped pale with cheer. He watched Corey hang his big arms across

31

the table, scooping up biscuits, bacon, jelly, shakers, butter—absorbed in piling his plate like when he was a kid. Pop was pushing bowls of grits and eggs toward him, laughing—"Eat, boy! Eat!" We got tickled.

Corey swallowed down a biscuit, a fork trembling in his hand, then said, "You finally sell them cows, Pop?"

Pop's eyes went flat for a moment. He had sold the Holsteins and given up the dairy racket five years before Corey left. He was visibly stung.

"Corey!" Mother said, pausing before she poured his coffee. "Your daddy's been running the hardware near twelve years now."

Corey nodded vaguely. He sucked some food from his teeth, and I saw the missing molar—saw it was a stranger sitting at our table. "How's that, then?" he said.

Pop raised his eyebrows, nodded. Over the last six years he'd had to sell half his floor space to a florist and let go all three of his employees. He ran the little corridor of a store himself now, and it'd been drying up for years. People didn't want much to do with our family. School was tough. "We're getting along, Corey."

"The store's fine, honey," Mother said, "long as your daddy gets his tail up there quick to open up." She pulled Pop's plate away. She knew to get him out the door.

But Pop kept up his dogged cheer, his stiff smile. We all saw the sour strain in his eyes—from being forgotten by a son; from the thought, too, of a few folks milling outside the store right now, checking watches. "Let 'em wait!" he said, leaning back for five silent minutes before standing and toasting Corey with an empty mug, grabbing up his balance books, and leaving us with the sound of his truckbed rattling up the drive.

Bethel

Mother and Corey and I sat there quiet. Then Corey let out a loud, unselfconscious belch. "Corey!" Mother said. We all looked at each other and laughed.

And that's the happiest part of this story.

All that afternoon, I sat on the porch watching my brother—a man no one remembers now, not even as a murderer—mow the pasture's highgrass. It was August, and though school had started up, Mother let me stay home. Corey swung the tractor hard down each row, sliding and gunning the wheels, popping the gearbox. Pop would've killed him. It broke your heart to see how Corey abused machines or clothes. Anything lent him was doomed to his subtle ruin and came back missing bolts or buttons hardly noticed in the first place, left with stains noticed only in certain lights—in every case rendered useless. He'd sweated through his flannel but would not take it off. Whenever he pulled the shifter, a shoulder seam gaped open on his back.

He was doing a shit job of it, grass finned and clumped in his wake. He always rushed hurly-burly through any piece of labor, impatient to be done with it. He was like this with living: his shallow, fitful breaths; his shaky fingers; his skittering black eyes.

After he finished mowing, I helped him stack the wood he'd cut under the eaves. Sister limped around nearby, but at a distance, glancing up at us—neither of whom she trusted—as if for permission to leave. Beneath her ashen face she seemed to remember Corey, to remember why she'd bolted home six years ago. Mother kept peeking out the window.

"Head to the pond?" I said. We'd finished with the wood and Corey was jiggling the loose porch railing with a mind to fix it. The mosquitoes were bad.

He looked at me, and what I saw in his eyes was: *What pond?*

The pond for which Pond Forest was named had no name of itself. It sat about a half mile into the forest that began across the dirt road. As kids we'd catfished there and sometimes swam.

I tossed my clothes at a felled trunk and squished down the soft bank, then floundered in. Corey watched on. "Come on, Corey. Cool in here."

He began to unbutton his shirt, his eyes roving the far bank. Over there a tornado had ripped through two years back and left a litter of felled pines, snapped off six feet or so from the ground. Corey got down to his grimy underwear and waded in. He went under, came up, and stood belly deep, staring off at those shorn trunks, his face nowhere close to being drunk on play like in the old days. The pond had always been a place where he could ragdoll me around without me crying, hurling me through the air with his long, loggy arms, his knuckles skidding off my ribs underwater in a way that hurt but only made me laugh harder. Today though, as I jumped and belly-flopped nearby, he stood there stirring water with his hands, blinking. He clearly didn't care much for swimming anymore. He was here out of some tenderness for his kid brother. I cut out the splashing nonsense and crabwalked along the bottom for a while, my head just above water.

"That's enough," I said. "Let's dry."

We slogged back toward the bank, him in front. I grabbed my shirt from the oak trunk. Behind us the sun lay heavy and cicadas sizzled around the pond. It used to be on a day like this we'd lay across that mossy trunk and sun dry. Exhausted from tossing me around, Corey'd splay his arms, let his chest bow out. His shunted breaths would settle into a more re-laxed rustling. As he blinked up through the leaf shadow, his mouth would fall open as if about speak from the depth we all suspected was there. But that didn't happen today. We both dressed wet and he followed me back through the woods.

We came out on the dirt road, in sight of our house. Pop's truck was sidled by the kitchen door. When I turned down our drive, which cut between the two pastures he'd just hours ago mown, Corey stopped and said, "I'll wait here." His shirt hung open. He stood there, staring down the road, which dead-ended into a neighbor's drive just around the bend.

"'Wait'? Wait and what? We're home." I looked at him, and he looked back, seeing that I'd seen: He hadn't know where he was.

He shook his head and followed after. "Goddamn, Pickle."

After dinner, Corey said he was feeling tired and headed upstairs. My parents and I sat out on the porch and talked cautiously.

"It's like he's not even my boy," Mother said, meaning it in a good way, a hopeful way.

"He sure has calmed down," Pop said. He tried to act calmed down himself.

"How about it, Pickle?" Mother said. "Good to have your brother back?"

"Yeah. It's good."

"It sure is," she said, starting to rock again.

"College of hard knocks," Pop enunciated, adopting the expression for the first time ever, I'm sure. He stood, gave a nod out our screen at the cords of wood. "Hitting the damn eaves. Look at that."

"He lost Skoke," I said.

Mother said, "Well," and kept rocking, as though it were a sad lesson for us all but one best left behind now.

Pop turned from the screen like he wanted to ask what did I mean "lost." But he didn't ask. He looked back out. He'd had an affection for Skokey.

Up in my room I found Corey sitting on the edge of his bed. I sat across from him, on the edge of mine. I took off my shirt. We hadn't said much all day and now stared at the floor between us. The window was open and I wondered what he'd heard.

"You and Pop won't forgive about that dog, will you?" he said, half smiling.

I shrugged. "Pop's a ghost now." I tossed my shirt at the closet.

"Nah. He ain't a ghost yet."

"Yeah. That, from a ghost."

He fingered his beard. He looked at the floor, then up at me. "I ain't a ghost either."

"I mean, it's like you're here and you ain't, Corey. You been gone." It came out in a rush; I could feel my face redden, tears welling.

"Hell, boy," he said, lying on his back, his voice seeming to recede away for miles. He looked at the ceiling. "I loved that dog. You all know that."

"You left him in the woods. *Skokey!* You *let* him get lost."

"Pickle"—he chuckled at my ability to feel tenderness for a dog six years gone.

"Well, you been gone. I don't feel much, I guess."

"All right, Pickle."

"I don't."

"All right." And he had the heart at least not to laugh at me.

It became clear that my brother was changed by more than

36

years. Even with a few good meals in him, that sick pallor wouldn't leave his face. His eyes, shadowed and narrow-set, seemed blacker, too black to really fix on anything. Inscrutable as cypress water. To see those eyes as I'd seen them at the pond was to understand the thin line between hate and nothingness. As though whatever burned in him for so long had finally carbonized. There was no point asking where he'd been. You could see he'd been nowhere.

That second night, I woke up and saw him standing in the middle of the room in his underwear. I was staring at him a while before I realized his mouth was moving; before I picked up the rapid murmur of whispers . . .

Fixin fixin fixin fixin fixin fixin fixin . . .

Corey missed breakfast the next morning. Mother laid out a spread like yesterday, but after half an hour waiting, Pop collapsed his paper and snapped the rubber bands around his balance books. He stood to leave—not without shooting a glance first at Corey's over-piled plate of cold food, then at Mother. It was a glance that spoke of his tolerance for womanish wastefulness.

Later, when Corey did come down, it was to sit on the porch. His show of doing chores had quickly run its course, as usual. I sat in the other rocker. Ignoring his smell, his dead-flesh face, I asked what he was going to do now. Inside, mother stopped sweeping.

He stared across the pasture, at the edge of Pond Forest. He shook his head.

"Well," I said. I flicked a mosquito off my arm. "You been places, at least."

He sat lost in his stare. "Yeah," he said. He yawned. "Worked up in Duluth one summer. Helped out some roofers. Saw Superior." He reported these facts as if remembering something he'd read.

"Pickle," he said, turning to me. "How long you think it's been?"

I said six years. He nodded. "Well, yeah, I been some places." He got up, stretched, and went back inside. I heard him slow-climbing the stairs and realized he'd brought back nothing of the places he'd been, only the heaviness of his body.

Corey's slow climb up the stairs that second day marked the end of his visits with us. He began to sleep through the afternoons. He must have heard Mother and Pop worrying out on the porch one night—about him still being wanted and all, about what problems were bound to come—because when he did get out on the porch he took care to sit on the shaded south side, by the kitchen door, so not to be seen by our neighbor, an old widower a quarter mile down who drove past our house every day to town. I'd come home from school each day and there he'd be, staring at his feet. Mother's face would be wrung out from trying to give him space all day. Corey and I didn't talk, usually, except for when I got ready for bed at night. Even then it wasn't much.

Then he rarely left his bed at all. The room began to soak up his vinegar stench, and I took to sleeping on the couch. He often hollered out in his sleep, frightful sounds that made Mother turn off the sink and walk out to the yard for a few minutes. Pop didn't stick his head in the room but after dinner each night, knowing he couldn't but irritate Corey. All week he left for work sullen and distracted, unable to understand or control this new shift in our lives.

Two weeks passed like this. One afternoon I was walking back from my friend J. T.'s, taking a cut we used through

Bethel

Pond Forest. The path took me along the pond's south shore, through the queer silence of those tornado-speared pine trunks. I stopped when I saw up ahead, squatted among some saplings of pipebrush, my brother. I saw the back of his head trembling, working at something. I got close and saw he held a slivered chunk of pine up to his mouth, gnawing on it, his eyes rolling back like I'd seen Sister's do tossing raw meat around in her mouth. Blood painted his thin lips; a rivulet had come down his throat, disappearing under his collar.

I stood behind a dead trunk farther down the bank. I don't know if he knew I was there or if it was someone else he was addressing when, dropping the chunk from his mouth to the pine needles, he looked up, his head gone still, and said in a flat tone, "Can't get the sweet out."

Then he lowered his head and picked up the wood with his mouth. I walked over and got in front of him and said, "Stop that."

He looked at the front of my shirt, gnawing still.

I slapped the wood from his hand. "Shit, Corey."

His eyes kept looping. "I can't—"

I slapped his mouth. "Get on home."

I never said anything about the forest business, but by the end of the week Mother had stopped saying how he wasn't her boy. It became clear he wasn't. He was sleeping around the clock now—hollering out nonsense all afternoon. *Ga ma heels! Ga ma heels!* or *Watch'er hooves!* or *Fixin fixin fixin fixin fixin!* In those rare moments he was awake, lumbering down the hallway, his old surliness had returned. Pop ducked his head into the gloom one night after work to ask "How we doing?"—*We done with this yet?*—and Corey, sounding strangely sensible, told Pop go to hell. Then he called Pop some awful, thorny curse.

For the next few days Pop went about his business, trying to imitate the simple economy of our lives before Corey'd come back. Then the following Saturday morning he
flung wide the bedroom door. "Rise and shine, sandbag!"
he clapped, opening the curtains and laughing. "Got to earn
your keep round here." He began to wrestle Corey out of
bed. "Help us out, Pickle," he called over his shoulder. I stood
watching from the hall; I didn't move. Corey resisted, but
with none of his former fire and spit. He was little more than
flesh now. Somehow Pop got him dressed and out in the yard,
where he had set up some sawhorses. Across them lay a bun-
dle of ten-foot two-by-fours.

"I figure Pickle can rip out the old porch railing while
you and me measure and cut," Pop said. He snipped the bun-
dle's twine with a pocketknife.

As Pop and Corey set about measuring the old railing, I
idly dangled the strange heft of a sledgehammer, and it occurred to me that my brother had at my age been far more
useful to my father, for all his hellraking.

Mother appeared in the doorway. "Oh, Lord," she chimed
with mock worry. Pop winked up at her from the yard. *Just
needs a good day's hard work.*

In the shade of the porch I began to knock out the
soft-rotted railing. Out in the sun, both of them were saw-
ing and sweating, Pop spurring him on every now and then
with a *Come on, now* or *Hold it straight, Corey, hold it straight*. It
wasn't half an hour before the adventure came to its predict-
able end: Corey clumsily miscutting and halfing a precious
length of wood Pop needed because he hadn't wanted to buy
extra; Pop spitting out an acid-edged "Goddammit, son!" despite himself; Corey eyeing him back and kicking out a saw-
horse as he told Pop to fuck himself before heading back in.

Bethel

After the scene, I stood by for a few minutes until Pop waved me off, saying he could manage. Which he did. He had the new railing up inside two hours.

I often wonder if my parents knew what was wrong with him. They never called a doctor to come by and figure whether it was tick fever or lockjaw or mercury or just a damned black widow. This was partly because we lived in a small town and Corey was still wanted. But partly, too, I think, my parents saw a doctor would be useless. Corey'd been sick in his own skin since birth. By Mother's account, he couldn't take loud noises as a babe, would carry on for hours after a mill truck geared past the house. Never could he be touched or held. I remember he always suffered sour breath, flatulence, and a feral temper. I can't name a thing in this world that wasn't hot flint in his side. He was a mean brother and I'd hated him those years before he ran off. But I don't blame myself for that now. I was a kid, hardly six. And besides, my hate was a kind of pity. I knew even then he'd never be happy. The stuff in him that for some people turns to love he couldn't let out, or in: it just kind of abscessed around his heart. Which is to say he didn't sort well with people. Or with himself, is the point. He's one of only two people I ever met who couldn't abide music.

Mother was cleaning Corey's dishes one night during his fourth week home, and instead of giving us her daily report on how he was doing, she said, "He's been grinding against the world so long, he's just ground raw." Pop ignored her, knowing she was right. Maybe they'd meant to get a doctor over eventually.

It was around one on the following Saturday, a month into his stay. I waited until Mother headed up to the store with a thermos of chicken-noodle for Pop, then walked upstairs and stood before the door to what had become Corey's room. No sound came from inside. I cracked the door enough to slide in, slipping it shut behind me.

Through the curtains seeped a dim, pus-orange light that gave substance to the room's heavy stench. Cutting that stench was a distinct piss. My eyes had to adjust.

He lay in the far corner with his mouth open, one arm hung to the floor. A lamp had been knocked over on the bedside table, its shade dented and dangling off the edge. Crumb-covered plates and cloudy glasses cluttered the table; dried food or vomit streaked down the two drawers.

A sound like a gas leak came from my brother. I walked over to the bed. Carefully, I folded back his quilt, finding beneath it my own, its patchwork darkened by sweat; I folded it back, too, revealing his hairless chest. The fever-heat hit my face like a furnace.

I reached back, took the knife from my waistband. It was an A. G. Russel 1861-style bowie. I bought it from the hardware at the break of summer, and though Pop sold it to me at cost, I'd had to save up a year. It was the closest thing I'd ever seen to a sword in real life. Pop seemed surprised I wanted the knife, but knew I intended no harm with it. "A pretty thing," Pop'd said, taking it from the case. *But not good for much.*

I gripped the knife in front of me with both hands, blade down, its tip a few inches off the rise and fall of sternum. His lips, chapped white, formed a small, perfect *o*. I lifted my arms, inhaled, and drove it down.

The blade clicked into rib as if into buried stone. The knife jumped from my grip, fell across his chest. He gasped.

"Mov'vug"—his arm wheeled around with casual violence,

catching my neck and crashing me across the bedside plates and glasses. His other arm came down on my head with the scrap of a curse—"vugger"—as if this is how he'd had to begin every day.

He rolled to his feet, pressing a hand to his chest; the knife clanked to the floor. I curled up and heard the door slam back into the wall. He grabbed up my arm and flung me into the hallway. He stomped after me, top-heavy, half spinning off the jam, some blood smeared thin across his fatty chest. Cursing more articulately now, he picked me up again and threw me down the hall, kicking at my stomach and hips, shouldering picture frames off the wall. He kicked me toward the stairs and—a banister leg breaking off in my fist—down them.

I raised my cheek from the shiny shock of oak flooring at the bottom and pushed to my knees. Still he was barreling after me, four steps at a time.

He threw me through the screen door. I again got to my knees and fought off the mess of boards and screen, then scurried for the yard and turned to take what was coming. But didn't turn fast enough. His callused fist caught me under the jaw, filling my skull with the squeak of thick ice coming apart and lifting me into a dizzy snow of light. I'd barely hit the dirt before he grabbed me up by arms and drove my body again into the ground hard as he could, knocking a terrible emptiness into my chest. I stared up at him, unable to breathe, feeling his arms kick with voltage. His eyes were black and unseeing. "Stop, Corey!" I mouthed, and then fell to soundless crying because I'd pissed myself.

By the time mother got home I was showered and changed. I told her J. T. and I had busted the door and picture frames horsing. I explained the bruise on my jaw the same. Pop was furious about the door, but didn't say much: I think he knew what was what. Later Mother fried up some catfish I'd caught that morning. She took a plate up to Corey's room, and the next morning he was gone.

• • •

Duluth, some roofers, Superior: my imagination worked on these facts for weeks. At school, at J. T.'s, at home, they stayed with me like lozenges I was forever pulling on—pulling on even in bed at night, where I was no longer given to comics or fantastical travels with my brother. Even now, all skin and age and bad sleep, I can't help pull on them still.

It wasn't long before a certainty began to sink in that when Corey killed that man (a man my age now) it wasn't for the reasons we all figured. Maybe it was a certainty of the sort that comes from being brothers, but I grew surer and surer that Corey's act wasn't any kind of righteous revenge or overspill of passion. He was just scared. Surely this ex-con fellow whispered in his ear what might happen if he told what he'd seen with the jacks. No doubt each shift at the garage brought glances suggesting this day might be his last. The man had made Corey afraid in the way only a child can be afraid. Fear did it, finally. Not righteousness. Not even meanness. Even now I am sure of this.

One winter he took a stone to Skokey's head after a truck got his hinds—this, given me on the porch one day, long after the meanness had passed into something else. He told me like we'd talked about it before. Like I knew everything about him.

• • •

It was three weeks later Pop and I found him. Fall had come, the sharp air, the cold rush of sun. It was the first day of deer season and Pop and I were making a last loop through Pond Forest. Swallows flew low eights over the pond, wing shards nearly cutting the quivered surface. Walking along the bank, I was watching them when Pop stayed my shoulder. I looked up at him and followed his gaze to a clearing. Then I saw him too, off past some ferns. He was lying on his stomach in the mud, knees knocked together.

I followed Pop toward the ferns, the world tilting with each step. Pop stood over the body and slung down the harness from his shoulder. It was a leather drag harness for deer. Its buckles stung into the mud.

He knelt, slid his hand under the forehead, and pulled my brother's face from the suction of mud. He loosed the rest of the body in that way, then began to push and twist it over onto its back—laboring against the stiff weight of his son with a helpless violence—the weight, the suck of mud robbing him of any last opportunity for gentleness. As Pop stepped around to the other side, I saw the face, tilted back and swollen. One eye was mudded in. The lips lifted away from the small teeth as though his mouth had been inflated with air.

I saw how small my brother's head had been. I saw the shape of a boy inside the man's coat of flesh—something you can't see in the living. He was barefoot.

Pop fastened the antler straps under the arms, then pulled two more straps up through the crotch, cinching them snug across the mid-flesh. His knuckles wobbled as he worked. I don't know if he could've done this were I not there. Finally we each took a strap, put it over our shoulder.

At first, we both strained against the weight, our feet sliding in the mud. He'd turned to mountain, my brother. It wasn't until we felt the body pull loose, heard the sound of Corey's back and bare heels snick across the mud and leaves, that we began to cry. Pop leaned forward, his small legs sliding weakly, his eyes and face purplish and crumpled in, tears coming off his chin. Me crying too, both of us choking out a rhythmic moan.

"I could've done it myself," he sobbed. "I could've done it myself."

Two hours later we walked into the house. Mother was washing dishes. A roasting chicken warmed the kitchen, filling it with the smell of stock and spices.

"Y'all get him?"—she meant whatever buck we were about to lie about.

Pop stared at her. We'd buried him at the edge of the pines, almost in sight of the house—Pop'd sent me back for the pick and shovels. In the end we left him bound in those leather straps because Pop couldn't bear wrestling them off. I could tell the straps were working on him now, though.

"Lord," laughed my mother. "You two got in some mud." She kept her eyes on us; her smile fell. "Paul? Paul, what's wrong?" Her voice began to get louder, buckle. "Paul, you answer me."

He was staring at the floor. He hadn't taken off his boots. He shook his head.

Then her face softened. She turned off the sink and walked over, drying a water-warmed hand and placing it on his cheek. "He'll come back, Paul. When he's ready. He just wants to say he's sorry. It's all he's wanted since he got here. To tell you that."

"Sorry for what?" he finally snapped, knocking away her hand like he had no more room in his day for sorries. He walked back out of the house. Without looking at my mother, I went up to my room. It had had weeks to air out.

· · ·

I sold that old place years ago. I left when I was seventeen to do some traveling of my own. Never did go back. Mother died of a stroke at sixty-four. Pop died four years later in a home up in Kirksville. I was twenty-eight by then, 600,000 miles on my rig, and both had been in the ground before I got word. I found the envelope about the property willed to me in a pile of bills on my apartment floor one night. I'd just returned from a two-week stretch hauling, of all things, Irish peat moss. I called, told some lawyer's secretary to send me a check. Told her I really didn't have time for this. I'd hoped it would be enough for a new rig. It wasn't.

Now I got over four million miles logged, most of them night miles I can't account for. Not anymore than I can account for what led my brother home for one month at the end of a summer when I was twelve. I can't account for the story of my brother, for what his life has meant to mine. I got no one to tell this ghost to, no reason for telling it. I had a girlfriend for a year once. She used to ride along on shorter hauls. One night, she drowsing in the seat next to me, I mentioned we were passing through Bethel, where I grew up. I don't know why I even mentioned it. Nothing but black out there. Maybe I figured she and I would be something big one day. She said, "I never imagined you had a family. I guess we all got families, though. We all come from somewhere." She rolled her head back to the side and closed her eyes. Peg was her name. But I know I've been driving too long, because sometimes I forget.

Last week I was night-sailing through the Utah desert—

which used to bother me but now just lets me feel empty for a while—and I stopped for this hitcher. He climbed in wearing a green army coat a few sizes big. As he pulled himself into the seat and shut the door, his arms trembled inside the baggy sleeves in a way that put you in mind of how spindly and pale they were. Right off, his smell hit me—a smell of charred bark and something god-awful dead. I was already regretting it.

"Reno far off?" He's your average hitcher, bug-eyed, greasy-haired, starving.

"Eight hundred, maybe some less."

"Well shit, man. I got to make Reno." He was staring at me, his small body cocked in his seat in a way that made me uneasy.

"There's a truck stop just over into Arizona. I'll stop there. Plenty guys heading that way."

"How far is *that*, man?"

"Hour."

"'Maybe some less'?"

"No."

He looked out the window. "Someone in that desert *shooting* at me, man." He turned to me. "Bullets spitting by my head like *hornets*. In the fucking *dark*, man, so I can't see where they're coming from."

His smell was working on me. I had an impulse to stop and kick at him till he was out of my cab.

"Some dude following me, man."

I didn't say anything, just drove. On the radio a guy sent out a song to his brother in Iraq, some rock tune about a woman dancing on a bar. The hitcher winced. "Can't hear you in Iraq, dummy." I turned off the radio.

I was hauling an illegal load of tar, hundreds of barrels of it. Some contractor tries to shave down a number on paper, and what it amounts to is me and my rig crossing eighteen hundred miles of mountain and desert, four tons over the legal limit. I don't understand how this world works.

A couple miles on, I pointed at the darkness out my window. "About there's Monument."

The hitcher looked at me.

"You know. Where they made all those John Wayne movies."

"Shit," he said. "I never went in for movies. Not for songs or any of that shit. I got enough on my plate, man. I got a feast of fucking famine, man. Bullets grazing by like *hornets*." He glanced past me, at the black window. "John Wayne. Shit."

Sure, he was alone, as alone as you can get. He was pitiable. But what I saw, too, was he was near the end. He's near the end and it's a good damn thing, I thought. He'd never make Reno. He'd be lucky to make morning. So what did I do? Thirty miles short of Arizona, right in deepest, darkest stretch of nowhere, I told him to get his bag.

He didn't curse or threaten me, and somehow I knew he wouldn't. He just shrugged, looking out at the night, his eyes pooled dark in the dash glow—the strained eyes of some nocturnal, ground-grubbing thing, worn out from trying so long not to get caught. Worn out from the dark. He hopped out just before I came to a full stop, and I was accelerating again before his feet hit. I didn't see him in the rearview—I looked. He must've started walking away from the road, maybe toward where he thought Reno was, trying hard as he could to fool himself. Maybe he was fooled. Maybe even in that blackness there was faith in every footfall.

My Father at the Mountainside

My father was a small man. I was ten when I inherited his cowboy boots, picked up years before on a business trip to Dallas and still new because he was not a cowboy and sensible enough never to wear them.

A whole Saturday I walked back and forth across our slick garage floor to hear those magnificent heels clop. I mouthed the word *gambol* over and over, mouthed it with each wide step, until eventually saying it aloud. "Gambol" was what the cowpoke had done as a child in the Louis L'Amour book, something I gathered roughneck orphans and runaways did. Gambol was not gamble but it was close, like junior gambling. My stride grew increasingly bowlegged and bandy, and the left side of my mouth stretched wider and wider around the word as around an accreting tumble of chaw. As the hours yawned I began to look and sound drunk, which I suppose I was, and I still had on the boots Sunday morning despite blisters, my cereal bowl sitting untouched while the garage filled up with more of that dogged clopping and muttering. I was four laps in when my father collared me into the car and drove to Blowing Rock, two hours away, just for the hell of it, or because he was tired of the noise.

My Father at the Mountainside

I pressed my temple against the window as the road cut through canyons of lead-rock mountain, striped from what he called explosive charges. When I said I'd like to climb one of these walls, my father pulled over, cut the engine, and said it might be a fine way to break in the boots—deferring to me as he would to a sensible old hunting buddy. I stood there in the highway weeds, a bit drowsy and stupefied by my burger earlier in Cherokee and nearly whipped off my feet by rushing traffic, and had only to walk up close to the wall and grope its massive stillness and raise my knee and skid a boot tip down the poly-planed convections and grit to know I wasn't climbing anywhere—a sad realization of physics and weight that stunned me out of the moment with a boulder-drop of bonafide depression.

My father crossed his arms and waited like a father letting me teach myself a lesson. Or possibly he believed, as I had, that the wall before us was indeed climbable, and climbable in cowboy boots no less, and this a standard method toward breaking them in, or breaking me in for that matter, he as senseless and giddy about the physics of fatherhood as I, in my shorts and boots, about those of mountaineering. "I got to talk to you, bud," he said back in the car, but couldn't.

Later we tossed a cellophane Ritz wrapper off Blowing Rock and were blinded by crumbs, and the day pretty much dried up. Our gambols in general pretty much dried up, as did that wine-leather luster of the boots on the drive home. I grew bored of them, and certainly they of me.

The Oldest City

I arrived in Florida three days ago to provide for a woman getting her Ph.D. in Laotian Studies. I like the dog park here. Her dog likes to run and bite the hind legs of other dogs. Really just mouthing. "She's just mouthing," I assure the worried ladies in dungarees. The ladies are retired schoolteachers and I have already got to know their frank talk, their worried eyes on the dogs, ladies both frank and worried, never frankly worried. I get it. I like coming here more than looking for a job. I'm here mostly. Dog park clothes are the best.

Four days ago I'm scraping Mexican off plates in some clattering kitchen way off in the outland slabs of west Houston, and today I'm departing a green dog park in Florida, nosing onto an empty sunny highway, my blinker blinking like each blink might be its tired last. Across the highway sits one of those unfortunate little brick bungalows trapped between a quick-mart and the intersection of twelve or so empty lanes of new blacktop that two years ago was a pine swamp probably, the complicated stoplight cycling two or three times before a car hushes by. "This little city's about to explode!" my fiancé says each morning, circling jobs for me with all her urban heart.

The Oldest City

In the narrow front yard of this bungalow there is a spectacle. A black man in a pale black tee shirt and tight pastel shorts swings a cane viciously at a red-tip shrub, handle first, as his little boy and toddler girl watch. He swings the cane as one swings a machete deep in the jungle—wide, shoulder-dislocating, murderous thwacks—rocking back on his heels against the force of each swing—sitting, nearly. Then the man pauses, stands blinking at the shrub, and holds the cane out to the boy. The boy takes the hooked end and swings at the shrub while not exactly looking at the shrub—loose flails that send the cane lolling around the back of his neck and nearly clip the vertical pigtail on his sister, standing behind. After a few swings she too is handed the cane. She walks around holding the cane like a machine gun, aiming it at her father, then at the side of their brick house. Her father stands close by, hand on hip, instructively observing, winded. A car goes by between us with a gray hairdo inside and glides through the red light, floating off into the distance as if swept along on thermals, and the man squints after it, his mouth wide and exultant and breathing. He looks back at his girl for a moment, thinking, then across the road at me. His mouth is still wide, exultant, breathing, but his eyes are as complicated as the word *ascertain*. I drive away from the dog park.

I cross a river whose name I have yet to learn. San something. There are always homeless men walking across this bridge, like they can't get off it. The homeless here are shirtless and tan. Then you get close and their faces are plated like a desert iguana's and they tell you it was better here in the eighties.

I don't go home. Home is a murky seven hundred square feet of brown paneling and three little windows crowded by dead banana leaves. "We live under jungle rot," I said yesterday, and the look I got. Then I said, "I bet Tom Petty doesn't live under jungle rot!" and laughed because an old Mexican I'd worked with in Houston told me Tom Petty lives here and the day I arrived I'd told my fiancé, who said she didn't think so and we'd argued about it, and now I was trying to make a joke out of the argument so I might head off a new one but got even a worse look.

So I drive straight to the beach and enjoy a fugitive beer at a café close enough to the ocean there's sand lumped across the parking lot. Twenty years in Houston and I never saw the ocean. I haven't still. I am here to fetch my fiancé's purse, left during brunch. I am dressed unforgivably, and I am happy. Clare, wet from the dog park hose, naps in the backseat on my fiancé's textbooks. The café will close soon, in minutes. Soon my fiancé will notice I am not back, or she will not notice, and I am now enjoyably at the beach, most of a beer in front of me, a purse on the bar. I pluck a card of soup specials and begin writing on the back of it. I write about my day more or less. I'll fold it up and slip it into her change purse. I imagine how her face will soften when she finds it, and soon I'm whipping an account of my day onto that paper with some real sense to it. I've never had so much to report. It's funny how the retired schoolteachers won't meet my eyes, like they can't stomach that I made it out of fifth grade. The part about the family is sharp. An overweight waitress wiping down the bar tells me she admires people who keep diaries, that her older brother writes in one all the time, though it turns out he isn't worth a shit.

I laugh, and I think, My god, some charity . . .

Charity. Now there's a name fit for a dog. Who the hell names a dog Clare.

I try to imagine her face again. I choke down on my pen.

The Oldest City

*One day do you think you could find some charity in your heart
for me?*

But when I write this part it ruins the rest. I pay with
quarters from her purse and ask where Tom Petty lives, and
outside after I toss the soup specials into the shrubs I hear
the CLOSED sign slap its little rebuke. I walk Clare out to
the beach for what I hope will be an orgy of self-pity only
to discover what a chilling thing the ocean is to stare at. An
older woman walks across the sand toward me, and I think
it's one of my retired schoolteacher friends come to tell me
that grade school is behind us, don't sweat the small stuff, I
see your dog is just mouthing. Instead I get lectured on leash
laws. I am ruining everyone's retirement. I drive home a little
scared of Florida and its eyeless marshes, already stacking and
restacking the minutes of my day like pebbles for the dreaded
evening progress report. Clare's head hangs out the back window, higher than my own, ears and lips flapping in the dusk,
her eyes steady and serene, looking beyond, beyond. My fiancé's purse sits on the bar. Tom Petty lived here in the eighties.

Unvanquished by the Dusk

Two thumps from the front porch: he was out of his wheel-chair again.

Rollsy remained on the living room couch some minutes, staring at his hands—his chief means of recreation since being tricked into a summer month at his grandparents'. Outside, another day moved off, trailing a syrupy light reserved for the play-wearied, while Rollsy soaked in the pastel pallor of their den. He tried to forget the noise.

This was the third time during his stay his grandfather had set off crawling down the front porch steps in search of a death spot more befitting. Had the old man his way, dusk's end would find him curled inside a crook of root, under melon-yellow ditch weed, or on a bed of creekside shale. Each time, he'd drug his feet down the two steps—thump, thump. Last week Rollsy's grandma ran out and collared him as he rasped his belly down the front walkway like some loose iguana.

"Your papaw's just took heavy heart since his legs went," she explained afterward, Rollsy shuddering. "He ain't picked up a club since spring, you know."

Not being able to golf had hit the old man hard. He'd laid

himself up in the bedroom, let the drawn curtains blue the scene with sorrow. He wouldn't even get up to see little Rollsy and little Marion Junior whenever their parents brought them to visit—though, upon being shoved into his room, the brothers were inevitably met with a grandeur confounded in their hearts with the far-spanning love of God; the old man sat atop the high bed, knees mountainous under the coverlet, and spoke at them from a great, snowy distance.

Once excused from his confine, the boys quick-pattered down the hall and sat through the gabble of their grandmother with silent relief, speaking only in the car afterward to ask their mother what did *regression* and *transgression* mean, and what was the difference.

Now Rollsy was stuck here. A month. Marion Junior was with the Cub Scouts up on Kings Mountain, having more fun than an Indian, probably.

Peeking through the column of panes by the front door, Rollsy saw the wheelchair—silvery and upright on the front stoop, undisturbed by the body that had leaked out of it. Also undisturbed was the white sneaker which, upon opening the door, he saw sitting upright at the foot of the steps, tied still.

"Papaw." Rollsy leaned from the doorway, noncommittally watching his grandfather drag himself into the yard. "Papaw." Where was his grandma?

The old man looked back, suffered to roll round on his hind end. He settled on his elbows and considered the boy. "I'm off, boy. Got to get me a good hide-'n'-seek spot. You tell 'em . . ."—he looked down at his feet a minute, noticing what he hadn't felt—the missing sneaker—then back to Rollsy. "Well, you tell 'em, boy." He grunted and rolled back to his belly. He lay there breathing a minute, then began pulling himself over the grass in small, weak heaves.

Rollsy shut the door.

"Grandma." His voice hammered through the house, setting china awarble. "Grandma." Nothing. In a voice like a shrug, he said, "He's getting away."

Rollsy looked in the garage: the Cadillac sat there, white and glacial, undriven for months now; but her equally glacial Lincoln was gone.

In the kitchen he stared at the phone, thought of calling 911. Then he sighed. He sighed with what he felt was very mature irritation.

Leston breathed in the earth. All the soft, sweet smells of nature broke down at this proximity, broke into hard and bitter pebbles of rot. Loam crumbled into rock salt, leaf mulch, worm crust. He pulled himself through the smells, all bitter as quarry dust.

Their custom ranch house allowed for no such decay—which is why he couldn't stay, not for a second more. He'd had it built ten years back, when, near crazy from being stuck in that backwood coon trap with his idiot son, he finally dug up the jar of money. He took his wife's arm and left Marion to the bog water and mosquitoes, foolishly thinking the boy too stupid to come after his due stake. Leston bought a lot and a country club membership in a private community two counties north, up by the Carolina border. The place had a gate even. But Marion, the tricky shit, out did himself, plucked up a girl from church and set her quick to childbearing. Leston was a granddaddy before the first paintbrush hit his new house, his destiny divided. He hated the South.

Quarry dust: he worked the quarries as a boy. Blasted out mountainsides. He'd like to have told somebody about that.

A few months back, just before Leston gave up on his legs,

he'd stopped in the hallway to notice a hairline crack running up the top half of a white wall and a few feet out into the ceiling. He ran his finger down it: it *was* a crack! A suck at the center of his chest told him how now it was just a matter of waiting around in that house until death hatched on him like an egg.

Rather than let him properly wither, the house would preserve him until the end. It would insist on his wellness up till that moment death walked in, dressed in golf digs, absently practicing his swing and chuckling about "the last putt"—this, the sort of bad comedy by which death is known here. *Nice swing!* . . . not even a divot. So, time to clear out. Time to live deliberately and rot. Cut his goddamned losses, before they cut him. You feel a tickle of the sickle, you run.

The old man had almost reached the far corner of the yard. Rollsy walked across the monkey grass and stood over his grandfather.

The khakis had ridden up his lifeless legs, bunched and grass-stained over a white calf. Rollsy'd never seen a shank so puny. He heard individual blades of grass pop under the wide-knuckled fists. It was a progress of inches.

"You said you was going where, now?" Rollsy held a pencil and Post-it pad, hoping to defer the matter to his grandmother whenever she came back.

"Listen to you—*wuz.*" The old man hung his head. His bald spot was red and beaded with sweat. "*Wuz, ain't, never-how*—your sorry daddy teach you no better? They not have grammar at that school, yours?" Rollsy's papaw didn't like to be reminded of how hillbilly Rollsy and his family were. He was rich now, his papaw—or at least compared to Rollsy's own daddy, who'd stayed in the same clapboard *his* daddy'd left him in—*his* daddy being Papaw, Rollsy knew, though he had trouble seeing the two in any way kin: his daddy had a lanky mope, and Papaw called him Mary—short for Marion, Rollsy's brother's name, too, and the last name of the wiliest son of a bitch their state ever knew, Francis Marion the Swamp Fox. Rollsy tried once calling his brother Mary, but Marion Junior called him a fat shit before pinning him to the dirt and punching at his face.

It never occurred to Rollsy to ask how his papaw got rich. But he did ask his daddy once how Papaw was so rich and they so poor. His daddy looked at him, eyes slumping out of focus in a way that showed how slow-minded he was, then said Papaw was once poor as the prairie but had some investments come through from when he'd been a hardbit Yankee. Rollsy asked when would theirs come through, and his daddy took him outside, debelted, and just clobbered him.

If his papaw'd been poor, he'd sure come up. He and Rollsy's grandma, Cochina—Mexican for red dirt, his mama'd said—lived in River Heights Plantation, which wasn't so much a plantation as a "community" where more old people lived. Everyone drove big clean cars and drove them slow. Lots of cut grass, lots of gardens and golf courses. Rollsy couldn't imagine anywhere more miserable.

"You coming in or not?"

"I'm off, boy." The old man was almost to the curb. Across the street was some thin forest, beyond which, last week, Rollsy—his belongings in a backpack—had heart-sinkingly discovered more golf course.

Dusk was coming in. Some cricket worried like a dry hinge.

"No use following. I'm history. Off to my tenement of clay, to the great re . . ." A car eased down the road in front of the house, the old driver waving as she passed, smiling at the cute scene. Rollsy waved back while, at his feet, the old man watched the car off, muttering about the primordial cul-de-sac.

Rollsy watched his papaw scurry across the street in a bone-scuffing scrabble. "Papaw." Rollsy walked across the street after him. He followed him onto the grass at the other side. "Papaw—"

"Dammit, boy. Get on inside, or drop a knee, one. I can't keep rubbernecking around every time you start up."

Rollsy looked back at the house, then at his papaw, all twisted up in his clothes and snarling at the grass, then at the woods ahead, which dusk left thick and black. Fireflies hinted something from the corner of his eye.

"All right, but I ain't—aren't—allowed to dirty these here shorts." His grandma'd bought them after throwing away the jean cut-offs his mama'd wadded into his duffel, but said they weren't play shorts. Rollsy pulled at the creases. He looked back at the house again.

The sky was spit through with bats. A good sign, Leston thought.

His grandboy was on his knees, following behind. If there was to be any measuring up in this family, it'd have to be him.

"That's it, boy," Leston laughed, crawling into the pines. "Kneel to the knell."

Among the trees, no light lingered. Windows down the street glowed amber, and even the green lawns stretched luminous through the dusk. But here in the trees, day was long exhaled. Leston felt an honest coolness—the dying gasp that surrounds the black pit of the present. In the now, everything's dying.

Behind, the boy watched his own fat hands pad gingerly into the gloom. Pinecones, gumballs, and other forest rot punished Rollsy's knees and shins while his papaw sputtered of the undiscovered country and blessed release. In lulls of silence and snapping twigs, Rollsy made known through intermittent half-whines his reservations about breaking curfew, missing supper, not to mention the play clothes infraction. But the legs dragged on ahead of him, one-shoed, disappearing around trees like some fat tail. Through the bleary toil and half-light, Rollsy kept forgetting whose legs they were, or that they were legs.

He had been duly warned about his papaw. His mama said the old slit-mouth was crazier than all get out; she—whom his papaw called Bob instead of Bobbie Ann—wanted his daddy to sic a lawyer on the money. As for his daddy, he never spoke against Papaw—Rollsy guessed because he was scared. Rollsy had to admit, both had a point. The things his papaw said to him and Marion Junior in that bedroom of his: facts of death as toothy and as queerly radiant as autumn. *Today, boys, I'd like to tell you about the Quench of Quietus*, or *the Recumbent Retreat*, or *Our Pale Blow to the Head*. Throughout his discourse, he made a scene of limply waving off whatever food was set by his bed, but there'd be hardly a crumb left when Rollsy was sent in later to retrieve the plate. Also, nights, Rollsy heard the wheelchair banging around in the kitchen, then the rodentile sawdusting of Triscuits.

But he followed him close because this is what grandsons did. And because it wasn't every day you got to see a man die.

Up ahead, Leston was discovering how the years of golfing and gardening had been a delicate thing: a kind of taxidermy, wherein sprite fluffiness makes you forget the ancient decay inside. They were all decaying, he and his golf partners. It was called necrobiosis. But golf was funny: the fluidity in the joints, the continuity of gentle, far-reaching

arcs, the fluffy fairway winds—why, there was surely a salu-
brious force at work. One failed to age so long as he had his
swing. Leston had golfed well into his infirmity. He'd been
hobbling up to the tee for several years. Last summer he'd
had to load a walker onto the cart to steady himself against
as he swung—and damned if he didn't shed a few strokes. By
spring, though, the grinding in his hips had him growling
through each swing. His legs got so bad he one day waved for
Orin Mobley to help him out of the cart. He played through
that hole, then told Orin, dropping his putter into the bag,
that he guessed he was done. It was a fine stroke of bravado,
but once alone in his Cadillac, driving home, Leston began
to heave and sweat.

He clawed ahead. His arms were all he had to move himself with, and they hurt. His right shoulder, especially. He'd
hurt it diving from a southbound near forty years back; awak-
ing in a boxcar, he'd looked out and spotted a woman working a dirt-road pickle stand, and her ochre skin made him
think he'd hit Mexico, so he dove. But pain, too, began to
decay, disorganize, splinter like an arrow, no longer finding its
way to his heart. His bones felt skewered through his body.

"There's a star," the boy said.

He had eaten nothing since hopping the car in Utica, and
she fed him pickles. She consoled his shoulder and his idiocy,
and he knew he'd marry her. "Use it wise," he said.

Rollsy was quiet a while. "Too late."

Leston nodded. He hung his head and let the pain in his
shoulder tear him apart.

It was night now for real. Rollsy could smell the dew coming
in. Around him, each scrape and twitter sounded cut loose,
circling through the dark like bats.

They'd been crawling a good hour, though Rollsy would've said four. He thought of his grandma coming home—from Bridge, probably—and finding just that one shoe. He aimed to put all the blame on his papaw.

Rollsy began to lag. His papaw moved ahead with a steady vigor. Every so often Rollsy would whimper or concoct some sort of grunt, but the old man never slowed.

Leston knew he had far to go yet, and he wondered if he had the grit. Whether he crawled toward it, or it toward him, either way the progress was too slow. Turtle slow. *The Tortoise of Mortis*. He didn't care where he fell, long as could feel himself rightly taken in by the earth and stomped to mulch. Some dank cavity of stone, or red-throated fox den—or one of those tombs of river mud eroded from the roots of waterside oaks. Maybe shush his way into some kudzu, become one of those curious lumps in the deep-pooled vine, shaded by the canyon walls it made across tall, dead trees. Kudzu, it rode south on a train just like Leston, seeds trickling out and taking over whole counties. It gives up nothing.

Each forearm came down hard before the other.

"You going to die soon?"

"Kind of thing is that to say?" A necrologist Leston didn't need.

"I want to go home, Papaw." He stopped, sat up on his knees.

"I know."

"I want my . . ."—the boy actually said he wanted his daddy. His *daddy*.

"This ain't no goddamn hootenanny, boy." Leston turned, fixed him with a look. Just a trickle, he thought, and the vine spread like holy fire. "We stop, boy, when this skull falls a gavel to the gravel." He'd shoulder-rolled from that train, and trickled nothing but sand ever since. He laid a weighty stare. "I *got* to die."

Rollsy sat on his knees. He started crying.

"What—lord . . ."

The old man rolled on his back and rested his sore neck, waiting his grandson out. When the boy didn't let up—lord, he could wail on like his daddy—Leston reached up, clapped a dirty hand to his shoulder. "All right, now. All right. I guess you need an explorer name."

Rollsy, crying still, looked down at him. He nodded.

"Okay, okay. Well mine's Swamp Fox, so you got to pick something else."

"But *I*—"

"You not want an explorer name?"

Rollsy wiped his eyes, sobered. "Crawdad."

"Crawdad, huh. There's your daddy's ambition, reckon. But Crawdad it is. Creek-hoppin Crawdaddy."

That got Rollsy.

"I told you so, Swamp Fox! I told you!" They had reached the end of the trees. "It's just more dang golf course."

His papaw squinted ahead. He pointed toward the far end of the fairway. "See those trees? That there's bonafide woodland. Runs clear out to York." He turned a wicked eye at Rollsy. "That's the maw of no return."

The moon was out; dew silvered the fairway. Rollsy looked at the wide black trees down past the yellow flag, then back at his papaw. "I ain't going in there."

But when his papaw lurched on, Rollsy followed.

Once on the sod, the moving was easy. The bristle was wet and firm, and as they squeaked across, flecks of it sparked up around their forearms, sticking all over. They half tobogganed down the steep tee-off mound, and Rollsy thought it was so fun, he got to his feet, ran back up, and came at it with more speed this time, shooting down the hill on his belly and skidding past his papaw like an otter. He could've done that all day long.

The grass was cool, and the moon held them like a flashlight. They bellied down the fairway, leaving dark trails in the glisten.

"Yes, sir. The maw of no return beckons with a slick and joyous tongue."

Leston clawed divots into the turf with sneaky joy. Tomorrow it would look as if some large, hoofed creature had stolen through.

Cresting the green, he looked back. His grandson's round head emerged from a sand bunker. Green sod-fleck enwhiskered Rollsy like a hobo. Leston was fairly hurtling the boy into manhood.

"I got to go." Not twenty feet into the maw of no return, the fear was on Rollsy.

"Huh?"

"I got to pee."

"Now?"

"I can't hel—"

"Lord, boy, I don't care. Just go off a ways."

Rollsy kicked his way through knotted bramble, cursing boldly—tripping over log rot and falling into saplings. Nothing like that other pretend forest. Worse even than the piney swamps at home. This place was a tangled and toothy mess. And black.

After offending a broad ashen oak, Rollsy tore his way back to the spot where he'd left his papaw, and what he saw there was not lost by the moonlight. His papaw was on his side. He lay there in the shape of a question mark, pants half down.

Rollsy was ready to call the whole thing off right there. The old man was senseless after all. He was crazy, and Rollsy'd let him crawl way out into the wild where he was certain to die, or get gnawed into like carrion. The flaccid haunches sagged down the bones like flour dough.

"Swamp Fox!"

"Go on, son. I'll catch up."

"But. I—I don't know where, uh—"

"*Git*, goddammit!"

Gravel shot sent Rollsy a ways into the forest, where he fell to crawling, not knowing where he was going, and feeling like he might cry again.

"I came from the quarries, boy." The boy was sniffling when Leston caught up. "From the black rock of New York State. Bet not even your pappy Mary knows that." He wanted to make up to the boy, as well as show he was still a man.

"Those hills was full of dead Indians. We'd dynamite out their burials. It's where I found my treasure. My fortune." They were shoulder-to-shoulder. "I found this gun, Rollsy, this old-time musket. Bet your daddy don't know that neither." But the boy repaid Leston's earlier stoicism, hanging his acorn head and ignoring the bait of dead Indians and dynamite.

"I was sixteen the day I found that artifact—or it me. The boys working the charges had corked the whole north wall with glycerin. We hunkered backside a ridge a ways off and plugged our ears as the fella dropped the pump." He put his fingers in his ears and smiled fiercely. Rollsy stared hard at the ground. Leston sighed. "A mountain thumps like that, it'll knock your damn brain loose."

The ground was sloping down. The walls of a wide ravine began to rise on either side of them. The boy held close.

"Came a long rumble as the wall slavered down. We stood behind that ridge, listening, till a wide cloud of dust ramped off the ridge top and hung over us like a wave about to break. We stared up at it. Then pebbles began to rain, and we had to hold our hats and crouch."

He wiped his brow, left cool grit from his forearm. Sweat stung his eyes.

"The dust cloud finally did come down and settled thick. We all just stood there, calling to each other and laughing. After about ten minutes, when it began to clear, this boy Meeks hollered, 'Les, what's that?'—pointing next to me. I looked over, and there's a rifle, stuck barrel first in the ground. I grabbed it up by the hilt, easy as if I's the one stuck it there. 'Shit,' the other fellas said, and walked over." Leston was quiet a minute, seeing their faces—men's faces, he'd thought then. "A woman's rifle, we thought. The barrel was three feet or so, shriveled with some corrosion, but the maple stock was still smooth as its maker's caress. Then I saw the wrist plate. Engraved in a fine cursive was, 'For Leland Jacomiah Gander, Jr., from his Father.' Now anybody from upstate knows who Colonel Leland Gan—"

His papaw shut up mid-sentence. A tree trunk lay before them, each end stuck in the side of the ravine—caught in the craw of no return. The trunk bowed up off the ground, too high to crawl over, too low to slide beneath. They stopped.

"Let's see here . . ."

Rollsy heard him slap a hand to the smooth damp wood, then the other.

"The road to finality is—*fraught*"—he pulled himself up,

groaned—"with the . . . "—he sank back, tried again, growling—"*with . . .*"

His papaw's white hair trembled in the dark. Rollsy looked
on wide-eyed, picking his nose.

". . . the . . . *GRRRR . . . dammit*"—he exhaled explosively
and swung forward, hanging over the trunk by his hips. "Boy,
get over here." The old man draped limp as a tree snake. "Hop
to, now. Unhook me."

Rollsy got up and stood before the raised seat of his papaw. All he could think about was that dirty, sunken, moonlit
matter.

"Unhook me, now."

Rollsy stepped back and kicked the old man's seat hard.

"*Ho*-mercy!"

He failed to lift so much as stomp. His papaw was still
hooked. Rollsy would have to put some shoulder into it. He
stared at the sunken rear end and took a deep breath. He held
out both hands, palms hovering over the dirty pants seat. He
closed his eyes and pressed in.

"Dammit—"

The old man swatted back. Rollsy caught the marblely
knuckles on his cheek and fell sideways to the ground.

"Fore you start crying, now, you get up and you get me
off this *tree*."

Rollsy lay there, the voice coming from far off, and he
mistook it for his daddy's and scrambled in a daze to his
feet—"Sir?"—then leapt the trunk and took off running.

He found the boy curled under a bush and had to prod him
out with a stick, herd him back into procession. Still hot from
having to wrestle himself off the tree—he'd hit the ground
with a whimper, then lain there trembling, tempted to thank

God—he whipped insults at the fat white legs of his grand-boy. The boy should've run off long sooner, never looked back upon this crawl of bane. But his gumption heartened Leston, who saw in him none of Marion's bandy pusillanimi-ty, nor the swampy sloe-eyes of the mama and brother. Maybe he'd bring hell sure enough. Leston sidled up to his grandson. "Know what happened to that gun?"

"I wish you'd on and die," he coughed, a cry in his throat.

Leston started to shake his head, then dropped it in something like a nod. If only he still had the gun. He'd give it to the boy. But he didn't have it. What all he did have, he had for not having that gun. If he had it, though, he'd give it to Rollsy.

Squeaky crying escaped the boy, and some drool. Leston cleared his throat.

"Meeks said I could get money for it. Sent me and the gun to this Civil War Commemorative museum up in Pike. $3,500 they gave me."

The boy tried to move ahead, but Leston clamped one of the fat chugging legs. A sore moan rolled forth.

"I stayed drunk three days, then broke into the little museum and stole it back."

"I'm *tired*, Papaw!"

Leston, his voice splitting into whispers, told then about what else he took from the museum, from the same display case. The glass picture plate was unclouded and revealed against firelight the yet-to-be Colonel Gander holding up his squirrel shooter while himself being held up by the man Leston guessed smithed and carved the gun, Leland Gander, Sr., one hundred and thirty years before the gun shot from an Indian grave, flew half a mile into the air, and stuck in the dirt by Leston's feet. "We rounded that ridge and saw sky where once was rock, and me there spinning that gun like I was John Wayne—like it was my destiny that had clobbered that mountain. What a joke! "

Rollsy tried to crawl away, but each time felt his leg snared by that root-cold grip..

Leston talked on—talked even as a gut sob spilled from his grandson, even as his own shoulder gave and he staggered against the boy. How'd he ever swung a quarry sledge, or a golf club for that matter? His arms quivered. When they gave, he'd be done.

They heard a creek ahead. Leston felt its coolness. He could smell it.

"And what'd I do then, boy?" He huffed a voiceless laugh. "I took my leave of the North and hopped a boxcar to Atlantic City, and there sold the gun and the picture to an Italian Civil War hound for near a million bucks." The boy was crying hard.

He'd have given it to Rollsy. He'd show him how to pack the gunpowder. Let him set those backwoods around the old house whistling with musket. Mary and Bob diving for cover. The forest filling with smoke and ululation.

They lay on the bank a while, Rollsy gone quiet by the loud water. They watched moonlight ribbon down the creek.

"Weren't for the moon, we'd just be voices," his papaw said.

Leston felt water rope over his calves and arms as they crossed. His hands whitened beneath him. At the other side, he dropped onto the clay, shivering.

"Swamp Fox." Rollsy pushed at his side. "Swamp Fox, get up." His papaw lay on his belly, cheek to the mud, sliding slow back toward the water.

"Papaw—"

The old man clambered up quick and was on top of him, the hands wide and tight across Rollsy's collarbones. His papaw snapped a curse into his face, teeth bared, nose whistling. Rollsy smelled the sour breath.

"Indians killed that boy! But I took my million magnarinis and dove at what I thought was *Mexico*." The old man's heart tapped through the soaked shirts. "I took that girl by a creek, my chin singing with pickle juice, and made her watch me bury a pickle jar full of Grover Clevelands. Not two miles from this fortune I hammered up a home fit for no one, lost one boy to fever, and treated the other like shit."

The creek ran loud over the small words.

"I'm not apologizing!" He shook Rollsy against the clay. "Goddamn *Mexico*, son!"

Tear them apart, Leston thought. Wipe 'em out, kid.

He let go the small shoulders. He was sliding off the boy, sliding down the bank, toward water.

Rollsy pulled hard at the soaked shirt. But still he felt the old heavy body slicking down the mud—felt, finally, how heavy that sorry body was. The other shoe bobbed white down the creek. Rollsy begged, choking on sobs. Pulling.

"I know, boy. Let go."

"Please."

"Let go, now."

But Rollsy pulled, feet sliding.

"I said let go—I'm coming." The old man rolled on his back, his face knuckled at the sky. "I can't do this with you here."

But the boy was gone—already across the creek and lost to its sound.

Wolf Among Wolves

My sister was living up the lake in a town called Trumans-burg. It's a good many uphill miles from Ithaca and I've always avoided driving there in winter because the road isn't safe. It's not so much the drive up as the drive back down, how even at the slowest speed, at the slightest coast, the car's weight can shiver sideways and slip queasily loose. Last time I drove up there was February. Clare called saying she'd killed her husband Pete. I told her call an ambulance and pulled on a coat over my pajamas, not without some worry over the drive.

For as long as I knew him Pete played guitar for one of those old-time quartets Trumansburg is known for. In high school my friends and I'd motor up the hill to where some farmer kept a still in his cheese cellar and Clare always caught a ride up for the weekend barn dances, where Pete strummed for hours and where I guess she met him. Clare used to say he was famous but I saw little evidence of this. He was well known around Trumansburg, a local boy in a town where it seemed everyone was a musician, shiftless and unhappy, hippies gone grim from too many long winters. In the first years of their marriage Clare would get me up there occasional Saturdays to watch Pete's group play in a café that never managed to get its liquor license. Clare brought a paper bag full of strawberries for the shine that got passed around. I bounced their baby Micah on my lap and Pete hammered wild on the guitar all night, curled around it so his black hair brushed the strings. But in these old-time quartets the guitar seems to me the least pronounced; I could hardly hear him beneath the fiddle, banjo, and bass. Or maybe I could and I just don't understand music. I never took Pete very seriously. I didn't think he could be much of a father to their son. Micah is eight now and has already developed the endearing knobbiness of his father. The same crow wings of hair. Pete's harder years left him more fifty than forty.

By the time Micah had started talking I was teaching math at Ithaca Junior High and visiting less. The drives up had begun to make less and less sense. I tried to go up Thanksgivings. They almost never came down the lake, not unless Pete had a gig at one of the college bars in town. That wasn't ever my element though, so I didn't go see him. Twice a year or so I'd call over to the elementary school and ask Doris to bring Micah an ice cream during lunch. Doris works in the cafeteria, and my father used to ask her to do the same when I was there.

The night Clare called it was below ten out. The street held so still as I scraped my windshield there seemed a kind of suction in the air, an echolessness, something like how I imagine space feels. The constellations held stiff as crystal. It was two a.m.

The road up was plowed and salted and I drove just a little faster than I should've, letting my mind go empty so that I could bear up against the scene at Clare's. Our folks have been gone years, and it surprises me now to think how little my sister and I actually saw each other anymore. It still surprises me, some, that I was the one she'd called.

On the phone she said she'd swung his guitar at him and a piece had stuck in his head. This sounded ludicrous to me. As with all of her dramas, it was difficult to hear beyond the comical. "He had a gig over in Watkins Glen where he knows I hate the drive, but later I drive over anyway for some reason and when I look in the window it's not him playing but some brick shithouse Louisiana fiddler with a oily ponytail, all these idiots clapping. He was at her house, Slim—I drove over. His truck there in her drive naked as June. I didn't know what to do but to go home and wait in the den. It's hours and he comes in sweet-smiling and I take his case from him and pull out his guitar. 'Neck's cold,' I say, and it was, like ice from sitting in his truck all night. Must've been half froze when I swung it. There's a lot of blood here, Slim, Jesus. Jesus, Jesus."

I told her hang up the phone and call an ambulance and she said fine but she was going to run over to the vet's house, about a mile off. She needed help, she said.

Twenty-five minutes later I was turning in to their drive, a narrow crush in the snow bank along an otherwise empty highway. I parked behind his puny pickup with the oversized freezer he'd mounted on the back so he could sell organic chickens at the weekend market: my headlights blared for a moment against the rust and faded ice cream stickers. The pickup had Clare's car blocked in. When I got out of my car I was surprised by the silence. I often am, up there. I figured the ambulance had come and gone and I'd be lucky to find anyone there. I followed the freezer's extension chord up the walkway and stoop; it snaked up and in through the sill of a curtained dinette window. I could feel the sheet of warm air. I couldn't help shaking my head.

Jacob White

I gave two soft knocks on the pane, then entered the kitchen door. Pete was sitting at the dinette table. His sloe eyes looked up without the ironical brow pitch I was used to. A small jagged sheet of wood fanned up from his head along where he parted his hair. It looked almost natural—the flap of unruly hair that greets us in the morning. Part of me saw this as just another symptom of how he managed his life.

"Son, you got a head full of wood there." I flipped on the porch light so the ambulance could find us. I wasn't prepared to be the first one here.

"Your sis gone out in the snow, nothing but her slip." The eye closest to the wound had a slight stigmatism. I noticed, too, some blood caked deep in his black hair; could see where she'd wiped his forehead. "I guess that's what she done. Her boots and coat is here still."

"She ran up to the vet's, Pete." I sat down at the table. "Get you some help."

"I mean, I sit up from the floor and she's gone, and my guitar's busted to hell. Kicked in." This seemed some musician's shorthand for the ultimate callowness. "I don't really know where she is." He said this as if about to cry. I realized then that he was angry. I'd never seen Pete angry. He was angry he didn't know where she was. He was angry at the confusion because he didn't yet realize it was he who was confused.

"She's just up at Dick's, Pete." I jostled his hand.

He stared at me, my words already lost in the blacks of his eyes.

I looked over his shoulder and saw through a doorway and beyond the darkened dining room the odd upward glow of the den, where a lamp had been knocked over. The mantle was swiped clean. The old sepia photographs of Clare's and my folks, the clock, the pewter candle holders, his great-grand-dad's Swedish fowler—all lay scattered on the floor some-where. A piano bench lay toppled, shorn of one leg. I saw sparkles of glass.

"Micah around?" I said.

He nodded and put his hand to the black pane. "Feel this, man. Cold. But, like, alive cold." Then I noticed the bench leg, lying next to him on the table. I reached over and took it, set it on the floor by my chair. He didn't seem to notice.

I stood up. "I'll go up make sure he's asleep." I walked over in front of him. I put my hand on his shoulder, which I was for some reason terrified of doing, and told him to stay put. Then I headed into the dark dining room and up the stairs.

As usual all the lights in Micah's room were off except for a flexible plant light. He lay on the floor under its blue-white tent, staring deep into an open book of dinosaurs. He wore blue pajamas and lay perfectly still, his face adult with concentration. Whenever I came to the house I made Micah kiss me on the cheek because he was shy and it embarrassed him. He'd wipe his lips and say "That prickled," meaning my whiskers. I'd tease him about how hard I was going to make it for him when he got to junior high, and after he figured out I was kidding it made him laugh.

"That grow light's making you stretch."

He looked up, startled. His eyes blinked into tired focus. He hadn't known I was here. He stood up and walked over with the open book in his hand. He stretched back the other arm and yawned, then stood looking up at me. "I'm supposed to be asleep."

"I know you are. Why aren't you?" I thought of the ruckus that must've waked him, hoping he'd discerned little of it.

"Those are pajamas," he said, pointing at mine, tucked into my boots. He was amazed, delighted. "You got pajamas on."

"You too. Now give me a hug and get in bed. It's three in the morning."

He put his face in my side and reached an arm around me, still dangling the dinosaur book with the other.

Downstairs I found Pete's chair empty. The kitchen door was open and a windless cold had overtaken the bottom floor. Pete was sitting out on the snowy stoop.

"He's out here," he said as I walked out behind him. "Somewhere. I saw him."

"Saw who?"

"That one that looks like me. Sneaking around under the snow. Under those bushes there. Soon he'll crawl up the porch. Try to sneak back in." Fog puffed thinly from his mouth. I noticed he had the piano bench leg back in his lap, clutching it.

He looked up at me. "I'm going to bust its head, Slim. Kill it." But he couldn't keep a straight face. He chuckled—at himself, it seemed. It was as if he didn't quite believe himself. He'd always been a meek guy, always given this same apologetic laugh whenever Clare had called me over to fix something. Clare and I often agreed that he was in most ways a child.

"Okay, killer. Let's get inside. I'm turning solid." I took his arm and he rose and followed me in and sat back at the table. I took the bench leg from his hand, stepped out on the porch and slung it at the woods.

At this point I was worried most about my sister, who I pictured running barefoot through the mile of snowdrift forest between their house and the horse vet's. I'd find out the next day this never happened. That she'd taken off the other way, running downhill toward the lake, through the steep of pines and powder and out to where the ice stopped, and couldn't help loosing a whoop as she hit the heavy water. Enough at three in the morning to wake some lakeside retiree who came shuffling out onto the ice in time to snatch up her arm just as she'd pulled herself out. He knew who she was—knew our folks, maybe—and slapped her. He put a coat around her, took her up to his trailer. She cried for an hour before he finally made out she'd killed her husband, which is when he phoned the police, fetched a shotgun from his bedroom, and sat back down opposite her in his recliner. She fell into me sobbing with this story the next day when I picked her up from the police station. I wasn't much surprised by any of it.

Pete was pushing salt around the tabletop with his fingertips, muttering some ballad about strawberry wine. It had been about twenty minutes and no ambulance or even police had arrived. And then I got to thinking I'd better put in a call myself.

As I was on the phone Pete stood and walked out of the kitchen. I was struck when I saw the back of his denim shirt, soaked in blood, a great tribal gush of it, reminding me again that something larger was among us, that this night was a shelf we were all about to slide off. He disappeared into the darkness of the dining room, where he seemed to be standing still. The room's hard surfaces resounded with a cough.

The dispatcher told me no one had called, that an ambulance was on the way, that I shouldn't try to remove the object, that the victim should remain immobile. The victim. The word reminded me of how all this would be written up tomorrow.

I hung up and walked into the dining room just as Pete was heading up the stairs. I followed him up. His arm stiff on the banister, he lifted his right leg higher than he needed for each step. I told him it was best if he stayed sitting. He said nothing. I said, "Pete." I don't think he knew I was there.

We went into the bathroom and Pete sat backwards on the closed toilet seat. He lifted the tank's lid, set it aside, and reached down to fix the stopper and chain. He replaced the lid, stood, then turned sideways so to get by me and walked out.

In the bedroom he made his and Clare's bed. Then I followed him across to Micah's room. Micah still lay on the floor under his lamp, not looking up as Pete stepped over him and began to make his bed too. I was surprised by the expert tugs at Micah's Star Wars comforter that told me he'd done this before. His shirt cuffs were still wet from the toilet and his fingers left faint pink smudges where he touched the sheets.

As Pete leaned over the bed his head cast an absurd shadow on the wall—a Roman soldier, a punk rocker. Micah gave a habitual glance back, squinting from his tent of light and seeing, it seemed, nothing.

Pete stepped back over his son, walked out of the bedroom and down the hall. He sat down on the top stair and vomited, then stood up. He had some trouble getting down the stairs. I sidled next to him, my arm around his waist.

We veered away from the funhouse-lit den and back toward the kitchen. He stopped at the dining room table, which, in the darkness, seemed a depository for years of unpaid bills. He took up one of these bills and walked into the kitchen. He sat back at the dinette, placed the bill face down, and began writing on the back of it, his hand pencil-less, his words invisible. For five minutes I watched the beak of his fingers hover across the page as happens when we're trying to figure out how to begin.

Wolf Among Wolves

"What you writing there, Pete?"

No answer. I watched him a while longer.

Then I decided I should go bring Micah down. Maybe it was a bad idea. But it was his father, after all, and it was maybe now or never.

Heading up I noticed a few dark dimes of blood on the stairs.

"Come on down and visit a bit," I said into his doorway. "Long as you're up."

Micah squinted, then got up and walked over to me, looking now heavily sleepy. He allowed himself to be picked up and carried downstairs. As we walked into the kitchen I held his head into my neck so he wouldn't see the back of Pete's shirt. I sat him at the table, in the chair between his father and me. "Uncle Slim's got on pajamas," Micah said. Pete seemed to be staring at the backs of his hands. He didn't acknowledge either of us. Micah stared up at him. At his head, his face, his head again.

I should have prepared him somehow. I should've told him what he'd see.

"Micah," I said. I didn't know how to finish. He wasn't listening.

We sat there.

After a while I got one of Pete's nonalcoholic beers from the fridge and sat back down. "You know any jokes?" I asked Micah, popping the tab.

Micah nodded and sat up in his chair. His eyes were holes. He put his hands in front of him, interlocking them in a sort of shadow hawk, then popped off his thumb and put it back on. I widened my eyes and he jerked his hands back under the table, smiled, and swung his legs, looking at his father, then back at me. Pete was mouthing something to himself. I asked Micah to show me again, and he did, more slowly this time, showing me the stubbed knuckle, the thumb he held in the fingers of the other hand—working hard to hold his hands just right so I couldn't figure out the trick. I asked him to show me how.

Some minutes later the sheriff shuffled into the kitchen without knocking. He was in a parka and jeans and looked about as tired as the rest of us. He was near sixty and his hair stuck out wild when he pulled off his knit cap. I was giddy with exhaustion and nearly laughed. Micah did laugh. The sheriff glanced at Micah as he walked over and took Pete's head in his hands, holding him with his fingers by the chin and the nape, peering thoughtfully into the wound. Then he pulled out a penlight and leaned across the table between me and Micah, on his elbows, holding the light into each of Pete's eyes.

"Ambulance right behind me," he said, clicking off the penlight. "Cayuga Medical's socked in. Said it'd be faster to send one up from Schuyler. But I don't know."

For some reason Pete's face turned bright red and began to spill tears. "I don't know where she is," he said. "I'm sorry." Then as quickly his face went blank again.

The sheriff looked at me for the first time, eyes squinted behind his glasses. "You got somewhere to take the boy?" He tilted his head at Micah, who stared into his lap.

I nodded and took Micah upstairs. In his bedroom I gathered up his parka and school books, and together we went through his drawers, putting clothes in a duffel.

When we came back downstairs the sheriff was squatted in the wrecked den. He'd turned on the overhead and was staring at what I hadn't seen before, a long sticky lake of

Pete's blood. Nearby was the busted chaff his mahogany guitar—a papery thing of laminate and wire. He exhaled. "Ahh Pete." Again I was careful to keep Micah's face against my neck. We headed toward the kitchen.

Only as I turned away from the living room did I become aware of the smudges across its walls—the ones that told how he'd swiped the mantle and wheeled swinging through the room, a life's worth of anger risen up in him and in a short minute spent. The thought of it filled me with an unexpected sweep of fear and helplessness. My chest had begun to flutter, and as I walked through the dark dining room I held fast to the back of Micah's head, pressing his face hard into my collar.

In the kitchen I saw the sheriff had put a woolen plaid blanket over Pete's shoulders, something I should've done. His dad's back covered, I set Micah down in the doorway. But something kept us from walking in. Pete was leaned into the wall; the good side of his head rested against the pane. Its reflection showed the little wing of wood. It was clear he had died.

Trying to sound casual, I called into the den—"I guess we're off." I was already guiding Micah toward the door.

"I got it. You all get on down the hill."

At the door, though, I stopped and looked back at Pete. I took Micah's duffel and told him to hug his dad goodnight. The boy walked over and hugged him without looking at his face, the way kids do when they're tired, then dragged his too-big boots back toward me and out through the door, which I held open for him as I pretended to tell Pete good night buddy.

Walking out to the car I heard the siren—distant, quietly invading. I backed out of their drive and could see the red pulses coming up from the west. I was glad to be heading the opposite direction.

Later I would make a pallet on the floor of my den, something I'd done once before for Micah and that he'd liked. After a few nights, though, he'd start sleeping on the couch, and by spring I would have us a larger apartment, Clare would be in a home over in Albany, the house sold, and we would all of us know what it meant to become people we'd never have recognized. For now, though, tonight, no one knew a thing about what it meant. We didn't understand yet.

We rode down the hill together. The car was soon filled with asthmatic heat and the scalpy smell of old parkas. I drove slowly and watched for the eyes of deer.

"Help keep an eye out for deer," I said, "till we hit town."

Everyone here's hit a deer. You expect it. I hit a wolf on this road eight years back, the first I'd seen my whole life of living here. It had shot out low and smallish across the road and for some reason I remember the sight of its pinned-back ears just before I felt it under my car.

Micah yawned and closed his eyes. Then he opened them, said, "All right," a world of uncertainty behind the words, or maybe tiredness. Before us my high beams opened into a swallow of darkness. I began to think about what I'd say to the kid when he walked into my math class a few years from now. I didn't know what I'd say. I didn't know what I'd say when we got to my apartment. And whatever he knew, it was enough to keep him from falling asleep, and so we sat there together, looking ahead, waiting for the lights of Ithaca.

Maintenance

I had a wife almost. Then I had a cinderblock house with palms. I had a dog. At night I had the hours. The dog wandered room to room, paws ticking, until one night—a taut absence of ticking. I sensed the dog by the bed staring at me in the dark. Mouth open, tail going. I sat up to rub her ears and put my feet down in a half inch of water. I bore it for a moment. Then we both slapped through the house and out to the backyard where I could sit and splay my feet in the dry airy grass and look at what stars were still there. I was in my underwear, skull hooked over the back of a plastic chair, dog off somewhere.

Wrenches, I thought. Where are my wrenches? The Yellow Pages. Broken something. The water broke. The star I was staring at started moving around a little, like my pupil was greased and nothing could sit still on it. In the corner of my eye some other stars slipped around too, slipping outward. It was discouraging.

Here it comes, I thought. The great sliding loose, quiet landslide of sense. I was recently thirty-two and already demoted to the back halls of my life, the back offices. There were channels to addressing the water and I did not know

them. When did I go from being president of myself to being, like, vice president? And from vice president to janitor,
then to something beneath vocation altogether, wandering
the back halls and back offices, for years wandering? I had
been wandering these back halls and back offices looking for
some work to do but not really looking because there was no
work; the offices had been abandoned, file cabinets gaping,
desk drawers overturned on the floor. There was only the
wandering, this lurking around corners or more often standing still, staring down another long hallway under the drum
of air ducts in the ceiling.

This notion of back halls and back offices I had derived
likely from my little bungalow's brown paneling, linoleum
floors, and stained ceiling tiles. It had been I believe an office
of real estate, so an office in fact—my bedroom in fact a back
office proper in some dead year. Day and night my dog, too,
wandered these rooms, ticking across brittle linoleum, lost to
her own back halls and back offices or to mine. On occasion
we would meet in a doorway and try awkwardly to dodge
each other before turning back the way we'd come.

How long had we been bunkered away? This slipping
loose has *been* happening, it occurred to me. I should write
a poem.

The stars have been let go . . . of

But it was me. Me let go of. A person named Peanut once
let me go from this warehouse job and I laughed. It's inventory,
I said, you just have to show up. You can be drunk.

But Peanut was acting under soberer agency than he knew.
The joke was not his joke nor a joke at all. I peeled out across
the warehouse lot and Peanut watching just got smaller in
the rearview, and it was like in *2001* somehow—I had been
swatted into space, where nothing's funny anymore.

Maintenance

This inability to keep track of inventory—of boxes, wrenches—what I had thought a superficial confusion—gave way under those skittering stars to a real, foundational confusion. It hit me then: my brain was marbles. My talk the clacking thereof. This was permanent. The linoleum had felt buckled and curled under my toes, the water like lukewarm plastic. I was never going back in there.

Seeing stars so far off yet still undeniable. To see something that far off and at the same time to believe, to believe that thing exists—it drove me crazy as a kid.

Space!

Space and the stars slipping around in it. I beheld stars as a child. I beheld stars once on a cold Christmas Eve. They were very far and still. My eyes watered, my ears sang with cold. Everything was still. Beheld: what a still, holy word.

Where is my dog?

Out With Father

"The food was good, the service was bad."

The waiter nodded and was withdrawing before any of us quite understood Father's words, and Father went on with his story about Barney Mendel, resuming the lewd joke about Barney Mendel's wife that always accompanied stories of Barney Mendel and that the waiter, depositing the check at Father's elbow, had attempted not to interrupt.

The waiter was Greek and in his fifties, heavy with close-set eyes, and it was as he attempted to withdraw his arm that Father, also in his fifties, had softly touched the waiter's cuff, staying him until he could clip off the clause about Barney Mendel's wife, then leaned back, turned the full of his dazzling, melted blue eyes up at the semi-prostrate waiter, and said not uncheerfully, "The food was good, the service was bad," before resuming the bit about Barney Mendel's wife, then the Barney Mendel story proper—the remark to the waiter a grace note of sobriety that held it all together.

The remark was just beginning to uncoil in our heads—Mother's, Sister's, mine—as the waiter withdrew, nodding—neglecting to clear the dessert plates yet apparently unperturbed, his rotund and tautly tucked belly fairly whistling back through the dining room, head erect and alert to his duties, jacket flapping.

After all, Father had not said, "The food was good, the service bad," which would have been pettily dismissive. Nor was he boorishly emphatic: "The food was good. The service was bad." There was no tight, patronizing grin; rather, his face hung loose with an undwelling, collegial frankness as he barked gently, "The food was good, the service was bad."

Here, I thought, is a man who's won his terms with the world. Between his years of being crass and cunning and his years getting his corners knocked off, he's managed a square fit, plugged in firmly to a deep structure functionality that allows him to plot poor service in a long game that renders moral judgment and piss-anting useless and the problem itself but a bolt to be tightened. During the exchange, it felt as if the two men had stepped briefly into the boardroom of their generation and shut the door: *Let us move forward in this world*, one says over the conference table, to which the other nods, then lights a cigar.

Years later I was driving my father to the doctor and we passed by the restaurant, closed now for over a decade. I asked if he remembered taking me there for my sixteenth birthday. Reposed awkwardly in my unfamiliar sports car, he hung to the handle above the passenger door, straining to see out over his high-hung arm. He swallowed. "How those spics kept it going long as they did," he said. "The fish was poisonous." Then later, as the doctor was explaining the new dosage, Father interrupted, saying to me, "I'm not one of those people who remembers birthdays, you have to understand."

The Days Down Here

I begin, then, with the house. Before we moved in last summer, an elderly couple had lived there. They lived there over thirty years and nobody knew them. They were alcoholics, it turned out. They were *serious* alcoholics, insisted the neighbor as he told my wife the story. Not the clownish sort forever making spectacles of themselves at club galas, nor even the sullen kind one occasionally sees alone in the middle of the fairway, whimpering curses and flinging the weak quicksilver of an iron across the dusk. No, these two had been darkly focused on their affliction and did not distract themselves with cocktail parties. They were not neighborly. One rarely saw them: occasional glimpses of slips and pajamas and pale limbs passing windows with the industrious hunch of rodents. Then one day the old woman was floating facedown in the pool. She had tried, it was somehow determined, to catch her cat.

"This must be Hammond," said the neighbor, Ted, as I walked over to where he and my wife stood at the edge of our front lawn. I had been sweeping out the moving van. Ted took his eyes off Jean for a moment to shake my hand, and then continued.

The Days Down Here

A week later, he remembered, he saw the old fellow riding a bike down their street. It was sunny. It was spring, said Ted Forester, who had been out front spreading pine straw. He'd stopped to watch the old stranger—he hadn't seen him in years—round the corner back toward the house. Ted took the opportunity to wave as the fellow passed. But perhaps the loss of his wife was too freshly upon him, or he was not yet as reacquainted with riding the burgundy bike as he'd seemed, for he regarded the young neighbor with pale, clear eyes but did not raise a hand from the handlebars. He passed by Ted and, turning into his driveway, caught the curb with his front tire, fell, and split his head open in the gutter.

Ted's wife was crossing the street to join us. Now everybody could be introduced. Barb Forester asked where we were from; Ted, realizing he hadn't, flinched with embarrassment. Scranton, I told her. Barb nodded at me, then squinted beyond my shoulder as if trying to spot the road that had led us here. "Pennsylvania," Jean added.

"Pennsylvania, of course," Barb said. Then, carefully, "So. Retiring?" They were a good twenty years younger. I was sixty-one, my wife fifty-nine.

Before I could respond, Jean nodded.

I brought Jean down here because she had spent a lovely, lonely summer on this lake as a little girl, and because she was dying and I'd never done anything grand or foolish for her. Back in the forties this peninsula had been all pine and hardwood, veined by two or three roads of cool blue gravel. In one of the deep-set fishing and hunting cabins had lived Jean's grandmother. Jean often said the most vivid memory she had in life—and here sometimes she ribbed herself with a dry laugh, for she who never took nostalgia seriously seemed always surprised by the lavish jewel of this memory—was running in and out of her grandmother's screened porch that summer, myrtle leaves and lake sand stuck to her feet, her grandmother sitting on the porch mending winter clothes. She said that around noon the mourning doves came in like slow honey.

After our doctor told us the chemo had again failed, that the stuff had spread beyond her ovaries, throughout her abdomen and into her liver, I spent the winter phoning a Lake Wylie realtor from my office at the quarry. I used the grandmother's name to try to relocate the old homesite. Through this realtor I learned the peninsula had been developed thirty-five years ago into a private community and that property values were now falling off because its custom homes and country club facilities were dated. Eventually the realtor had found the lot—now a terraced waterfront property occupied, as it turned out, by the Foresters' house. But a house across the street had just come on the market. He mailed a photograph. The place cost everything we had.

Ted and Barb's steepled house rose behind them; through its many bay windows, the lake beyond it glittered.

"We brought our son, too," Jean was telling the Foresters, but they seemed not to connect this announcement with Zach, who walked up behind us shirtless, his pale, black-haired chest sweaty. He was wearing the gray Dickies and dust-white boots he'd worked in at the small quarry I ran for thirty years and had just sold. Zach was nineteen and handsome, but a bit severe in the eyes and, like me, new to neighborliness. He shook the Foresters' hands.

That morning we'd descended a Piedmont hill and driven onto the lake's bridge, concrete joiners galloping beneath the moving van. Jean, sitting between Zach and me in the cab, brought her hands to her chest and said, "Oh, there it is still," pointing across the boat-buzzing lake to the South Carolina shore at a peninsula terraced with half-million-dollar homes. She clasped our forearms, and at that moment I believed I'd done the right thing.

As if coming to, Ted Forester apologized for the story of the house's former owners. Barb gave him a hard look—*You told them*? (Many months later, during one of the weekly dinners they invited me to at their house, Ted brought up the story once more, again apologizing for it. It had just spilled out, he said. He hadn't known. She looked so damned healthy, he said.)

The Foresters walked back through their aggressively landscaped yard, Zach back toward the boxes in the driveway. Jean and I turned toward our new home and crossed our arms in a gesture of solidarity. The house sat huge and shutterless. In the driveway rested the yellow moving van, chalked with highway dust, and our trailered Monte Carlo with its salt-pitted bottom. Jean said, "Hammond, this house is too big!" and then broke the stillness of the street with one of her easy laughs, tossed aside like a dishrag, and I knew we'd made it through.

Our place remained from the neighborhood's first generation of custom homes: it was built of asymmetrical segments and its vertical siding was painted, like all the neighboring houses, some unnameable earthen hue—a taupey gray. The wide-lapping, intersecting slopes of its roof suggested the repose of an accomplished life, but its upkeep—the smoke-yellowed ceilings, the bathrooms' greened brass fixtures, the rotting doorjambs, the dead bulbs—exhaled many dismal years of resignation. And the yard? Fronting the eighteenth tee, the old couple's black tangle of a backyard had long blighted the crescendo effect the club encouraged along this hole. Other neighbors obviously took pride in the dramatic function of their yards here, and they must have made a point to spend hours each spring weekend planting verbena, dahlias, and geraniums, cropping cycads and imperial pampas grass, encompassing the tee within a sort of botanical stadium. But our house—there is no denying it—was a blight. The tree limbs were so dead as to look scorched; leaves buried the two back patio steps, scalloped the patio itself, and lay like a bunker net over the small pool. The rising shrubs made the house look as though it were actually sinking. Within days of our arrival, neighbors would drop by with cookies and express a frank eagerness for us to repair the yard.

Not just everything we had, but everything we would ever have. Yes, I begin with the house. With this story of dying elders. With the prospect of a few months. With the sight of our son stalking miserably through the calf-high lawn in his size thirteen steel toes, picking up toys left there by the Foresters' girls—eight and ten, and on the swim team. Jean standing before it all, loosing that old laugh of hers.

"What an awful story," Jean said in bed that first night in the house, the darkness around us new and tentative.

"It's likely made up," I said. "Invented. You know, out of some need to make it humorous. I mean, the old lady chasing her cat, the old man flying headlong over his handlebars—it's slapstick."

"But *brains in the gutter*? Who does he think he is, telling me such a story? I'm old enough to be his . . ."—she looked at me from her pillow, and I could make out the blacks of her eyes, thanks to a dull amber streetlamp. Cicadas whirred outside. Neither of us could sleep.

I waited. This coverlet chatter carried in it, still, the pretense that we were retiring south together. We were having trouble letting the act go.

I looked at the ceiling. "I'll stay clear of the bike."

"Hammond!" She began to cry. I kept my eyes on the ceiling. I didn't hold her. To do so would have been to admit to the darkness around us, to how far we were from home, to how small her body had gotten. To the strangeness of this place, its absence of history or hope.

I patted her hand. "Easy. We might all still be alive tomorrow."

But her fingers hooked mine in a hot animal grip.

Learning to sleep here took time. We were used to a darkness absolute and whispered-through by the wash of truckers across the valley, downshifting along the high ridge of I-81. We were used to our popping beams and the worrisome squeak of our porch swing and hanging planters, to Zach clearing his throat in his room above us—a cool constellation of sounds. But sound did not travel in this new house. A heavy cloy of quiet held the air, a pressure. Outside, locusts thrummed against the humidity. Zach's room was way off down another hallway. We were relieved to find him in the kitchen that first morning. Shirtless and sweaty-faced, he'd already mown the front lawn. It was the mowing that had awoken us.

We all stood in the kitchen for most of a minute, somewhat at a loss. Zach glanced at each of us uneasily and sipped water from a plastic mug. The distance we stood from each other across the commodious kitchen had, actually, the effect of embarrassing intimacy. The blank space asked us to define ourselves in a way our morning routine in the old, close kitchen had made unnecessary. "I got to get a job," Zach said wryly.

At this moment, tired and disoriented, I felt suddenly unprepared for this house and its spaciousness. A summer cabin up in the Finger Lakes would've been better, surely.

"Needs an island in here," I said, walking across the kitchen toward Zach, holding out my hand for the plastic gas station mug in what felt like a grasp for fatherhood itself. In Pennsylvania the green and gray mug had long been a source of competition within our family: its lid didn't leak, and we were always irritably retrieving it from one another's cars. It rode with us in the cab all the way down here, and all the sodas we'd bought were communal. "You got to do nothing this summer," I said, "but enjoy yourself." I sipped the tap water. "That goes for all of us. We're going to resuscitate this house, and we're going to enjoy ourselves." I took another sip. No such plan had occurred to me until I was actually speaking the words. But it seemed to make sense.

"Oh yes," Jean said, accepting the plastic mug, whose size eclipsed most of her face. "Let's party."

Later that morning, Zach and I raked leaves three winters dead into piles while, at the edge of the backyard, Jean swung a rusted machete at black vines and briars and chest-high weeds that obscured the golf course. She'd found the military-issue tool under a workbench in the garage. Sweat slicked her neck. "Easy, girl," I'd say every now and then. She'd ignore me and hack more fiercely—a petulance new to her character in the past six months, a desperation I didn't yet take seriously. This was only weeks before her cheeks sallowed and sank, before her eyes turned to pitch.

"Easy."

The Days Down Here

Zach walked over to his mother and, given the machete, hacked at a high-up vine she couldn't reach and then handed it back. He was a natural worker, and I worried about him here in this sprawling repose of fairways and retirees. Instead of going to college the year before, Zach had stayed on at the quarry, which pleased me for a number of reasons. But he had no friends, really; he'd been living with us. I guess it's something Jean never forgave me for.

There was no reason he should've come down here with us, other than *the* reason. His very presence was a reminder. Neither of us had long with her.

"Not looking so hot yourself, Winston," my son said, referring to me as he had at the quarry by the Winston Racing painter's cap I wore. Jean hated the cap. She would reach to pluck it off me first thing whenever I walked in from work, evenings, and give my bare scalp a sticky pat. Yet she hadn't chastised me for wearing it in front of the Foresters the day before; she'd only smirked up at the thing as we walked back toward the boxes in the driveway. She was letting some things go.

Over her shoulder, Jean said, "Go get some water, Ham. You're thirsty."

I did. I was.

In the kitchen my vision was splotched from the sun; my head throbbed from the humid southern heat. The plastic mug was outside and our glasses were boxed up, so I leaned under the faucet. I gulped greedily, though it was some deeper coolness I wanted. Like the sudden puff from newly split mountainside—"mountain kiss," quarrymen called it. Fills your chest like the cold of an ax. And even as I thought about the quarry, about how strange it was I would never again see that massive space, I felt a draft slip from the basement door.

Instinctively I walked over, opened it, and felt for the banister.

The basement was six hundred square feet with cinder walls. Two window wells limned the musty stillness and silvered its slick-mottled concrete floor. The smell of damp, iron-rich clay hung thick and frank. That afternoon, my face pouring with sweat, I clomped down the basement's unsteady stairs and found there a cool cofferdam beneath the heavy-lying summer above.

I would end up down there often, those first weeks—resetting breakers, installing a new hot-water heater, tracing the bowels of some piece of plumbing—feeling with each trip down the wobbly stairs some release from the quiet crush above, some cool collapse. A few things lingered from the lives before ours. Against the dark back wall leaned two bald tires, and I'd found behind the old water heater a damp cardboard box with arrowheads scattered across its bottom. But it was the old library desk I'd found that first day—pushed against a brick column, close enough to the washer and dryer to suggest it had served as a folding table—that made me feel, suddenly, that I was in someone else's space. A wooden chair sat shunted back from it, as if someone had just gotten up to check the mail. I sat; I ran my hands over the desk. It was large enough to serve as a small dining table, its wood dark from moisture, and its single drawer wide and shallow. The wood barked as I pulled it open.

A chaos of yellow legal paper littered the drawer, as if flung there in some drunken fury and shut away. A dark and deliberate cursive filled every page. Over the next half hour I collated the numbered pages. They stank bitterly from old cigarette smoke and dried out my eyes. I set them on the desk finally in a neat inch-high stack. Heading the first page was *A History of River Heights*.

The Days Down Here

When we look around us today, the text began, *it is hard to believe that these houses were not always here, that the elegant fairways of green did not always wend through our hills like a river. . . .*

And that was enough. It was pamphlet fodder for some historical society like those that littered the hill counties across northern Pennsylvania. But this neighborhood—it wasn't thirty years old! I mean, *A History of?* I neatly replaced the manuscript and shut the drawer. I sat there for a moment before heading back up to the patio. Pushing myself up, I couldn't help muttering, "Sad bastard"—words I would remember with great particularity a few months later when I sat down there trying to recover a history of my own, finding coolness aplenty on those long winter days.

Jean and I spent much of May working together on the house, trying to wrest it from its dreadful spirit of failure. The linoleum was peeling up under the cabinets, lumped with old golf tees and coins: we scraped it up and laid down some faux blond-oak paneling. We spent a week tiling the kitchen counters, another replacing two rotted-out window casings. We painted, replumbed, rewired. On days Jean felt tired I worked alone while she napped on the couch, occasionally calling my name to make sure I was still in the house. We weren't used to being together all day. After I put up my tools, we'd share a drink on the back patio, watching the last of the evening golfers trundle by. Sometimes we waved, and they'd wave back, confused. You have to picture us: two pale sixty-somethings, me with my painter's cap and plaster-fleck-ed forearms, Jean in her by-now-usual sweat pants and snap-front pajama top (both smudged from weeks of work), to-gether presiding from our chaise longues over a swampy moat of algae and leaves and up-clawed limbs. We never got around to the pool.

"I'll go by the hardware tomorrow and pick up a mulcher," I said one afternoon toward the end of May. Limbs lay piled across the yard before us, where we'd left them that first day.

"Not buy, I hope."

"No, they rent. We'll get this place palatial yet."

"Well, don't buy anything else, Ham. I mean, there's no sense in . . . in killing ourselves . . . at this point."

"We've put a lot into it already," I said, refusing to miss a beat. "Everything, really. We might as well get it exactly how . . . you know, finish it." We found ourselves dodging certain phrases, that summer.

"Yes. You're right." The pajamas and sweats guarded Jean against some private, persistent chill.

"Zach, though," I said, trying to draw her into more perennial projects.

"Mm?"

"No kids his age here, you know." It was a concern that had been hers, not mine—a concern that, like so many lately, she seemed to be letting go of.

Her hand lifted for a moment, limply took in the neighborhood, dropped. "They send them off to college."

A week after we'd arrived, Zach had gotten a job manning the gas dock at the club's marina. He worked every day and soon began arriving home at dusk shirtless and incredibly tan, dropping his old skateboard in the mudroom. We didn't see him much. I pictured him sitting alone all day in that shack, staring out over the lake. Sometimes when he came in, his cutoff jeans and hair were damp as if he'd been swimming.

A scrap-winged robin broke from the branches of a sweet

gum.

"I think you need to find something to do during the day," she finally said to me.

"To do?—oh, we've *plenty* to—"

"I mean on your own. Out of the house."

"What, like fishing?"

"Stop it. Didn't Ted offer to sponsor you? For the club?"

"Hell." I waved it off. "I ain't club material, girl."

"Just play some damn golf, Ham. Or go to the pool. You'll . . . you need to get out of the house."

"I do, huh?" I looked down at the funky pool water, shaking my head, and felt my face slacken with the stupidity of defeat, my lips pouting out some nonsense—"That's silly."

We sat silently through the final pinch of sunset, as we often did, waiting to hear the idle rumble of Zach's skateboard coasting down our street. How smooth the streets are here. When we did hear him, I looked at my watch, sighed, and dropped my feet to the porch.

Before I could stand, Jean stayed me. "Hey," she said, jostling my arm. "Hey. We might all be alive tomorrow, old goat."

She'd said this often over the previous few weeks—whenever, kneeling together over some project or other, she sensed my chest stiffening against an unexpected stab of grief. I don't think she believed the words, but I loved her for saying them. *We might*, I'd nod, *yes, we might*, as if that's what I'd been trying to tell her all along.

That night Jean went straight to bed after dinner. Zach dozed in front of the television, looking healthy and exhausted. I went downstairs.

Above the desk a work light dangled by its orange cord. Under its hot bulb I opened the drawer and again set the stack of papers before me. Within five minutes my scalp had begun to sweat.

Even as flatbeds filled the pines and ravines with gravel dust; even as the valleys echoed with the hammers of framers, and dozers ripped up the monstrous roots of oaks, three men with golf spikes and clipboards were teeing up on the red-clay fairways to test the course's playability, their vision for our community a clear and simple thing, finally. Fred Byrd was a renowned golf course architect who'd worked with Bruckheimer in nearly all of his previous developments. With him was Gary Kantz, the Charlotte Country Club pro, and L. B. Bruckheimer himself, who'd flown up from his home in West Palm Beach to walk the course with them, though he was seventy-six at the time. He was a small man.

Currently in the club's Roundhouse Lounge there hangs a photo depicting the three men standing on what seems a Martian landscape (actually the hole six tee-off!): it's 1969, and Byrd and Bruckheimer stand by with binoculars as Kantz's body unwinds, his one-wood flying down in a ghostly fan.

Golf was a disaster. I'd played Scranton's county course fifty times in half as many years. I had my own clubs, even. But I was bad at it.

After Ted put my name on a fill-in list at the club, I was called out of bed one Tuesday morning to square up a foursome in danger of losing its seven o'clock tee time. At the cart pickup, the largest of three white-haired men stepped forward, grabbed my hand, and said with the good-ol'-boy drawl of the self-made, "There's my *partner*." But this would be the warmest moment of our camaraderie. Throughout the day my drives veered into forests and yards and creeks, and twice my increasingly stoic partner had to circle the cart back because my skinny canvas golf bag had slipped loose from the back. We got clobbered so badly no one could enjoy it, so after eighteen holes all I could do was wander around the pro shop as the other men leaned on the glass counter talking and chuckling with the young club pro.

Along a wall at the back of the shop hung a succession of group photos from various tournaments over the years, going all the way back to 1974. In each, two dozen pleasant, jowly men gathered on the eighteenth green, the lake visible behind them. I moved backward through the photos, watching many of the same men grow younger, thinner, regain hair. I scanned the names and of course found the old man's beneath the 1980 photo. The name had haunted a number of forms the realtor sent to Scranton. I counted across the back row. He was taller than any of them, his head listing merrily with a wide, thin smile. His hair was mussed from a breeze, or from the long day of play. He looked then about my age. Younger maybe. I found him in all the preceding pictures, even in the inaugural 1974 group—he'd won, that year. First-ever club champion. He stood up front, thumb raised.

I could now see clearly his body flying off that bike—or collapsing, more likely, crumpling. Perhaps he'd put out a leg but found the last strength of his body shattered.

Outside, the men sat on the back bumpers of open-trunked Lincolns, pulling off their spikes. The one who'd been my partner, Orin, walked me to my car, obviously remarking to himself the rust-pitted fender. He put his hand on my shoulder and smiled down at me, even as his blue eyes hung with the morning-sogged fury of the elderly, and he said, "Next time, ask Ted to post your handicap. This isn't what we pay our dues for, friend." With a pat, he turned and walked back up the parking lot, his spikes grinding across the asphalt with plodding and dutiful cheer.

I dropped my clubs in the trunk and stood there. I needed to walk off some steam, so I headed back across the parking lot and up hole eighteen toward the house.

"How was it?" she said as I pushed like a prowler through the red tips. She sat propped in a chaise, wearing a blouse tucked into some jeans. She, too, had tried to make a day of it.

"Exhilarating." I walked past her and through the open sliding door, and in the kitchen fixed a drink. I leaned on the counter for a while, staring at the glass, then took it up and walked down the hall.

Again I found myself in the basement, sitting before the desk. But when I pulled out the drawer I saw matters had altered. My neat stack of paper had become two, side by side. The left stack was facedown, the right a solid block of text: page 26.

By 1970 the peninsula's trees had been thinned out for surveying lots. Asphalt roads had been laid down. The official groundbreaking for River Heights took place in the spring of that year down at Commodore Point and consisted of the demolition of an old paint-shorn lake club, the Goujon, and its two rows of half-sunk boat slips. On top of this site began the construction of the River Heights Marina. The Marina's completion in 1973 was attended by a grand ceremony of four hundred people and concluded with a pontoon parade.

The dryer spun behind me, our work clothes collapsing

and recollapsing upon one another. A penny or a button skittered about.

The sight of Jean in her old jeans and blouse upstairs had depressed me. The denim sagged over her abdomen. We'd been here over a month now, and I could no longer ignore the change in her body, in her eyes even. I began to think more and more often of our doctor in Scranton who, unable to dissuade us from moving down here, had taken me aside at the last minute and, clearly angry, urged me to make hospice arrangements as soon as we moved in. I hadn't, of course.

The drawer wouldn't go back in, so I had to pull it out and jiggle it. In doing so I dislodged a quarter-smoked cigarette from its depths: it came rolling forward across the cursive script, a relic of some ancient deception, browned and hollow at the tip where its ember had been tapped out. He'd come down here to smoke, to be alone. To work on his little history. Couldn't bear it up there, the poor bastard.

I swatted the cigarette back into its darkness and jammed the drawer back in.

Back on the patio I sat next to Jean, told her it had been nice to get out and hit the ball. I was ashamed of feeling depressed about her appearance, and of my petulant anger earlier about, of all things, golf. I told her she looked crisp. But as I looked over at her, I felt I'd missed some larger point, because her smile seemed, as it did more often now, miles and miles offshore.

I began going to the club pool several mornings a week. It was by now late June. In the bathhouse I would change out of the golf trousers I'd left the house in, and then sit at an umbrella'd table in trunks and a golf shirt and try to read a novel from the pool's paperback library. From high-hung speakers soft rock wisped over the pool like cirrus. Small, reed-chested kids ran off the diving board, their midair yelps snuffed by the water, leaving the board's dying clap. There was the tired, lumbering flop of old women's arms in the lap lane, the hourly pall of adult swim. And sure enough, here were Jean's mourning doves, pouring through the trees at noon as she remembered—mixed now with the faint whine of boats coming in from the lake, the drowsy waver of invisible planes in the empty blue sky, comfortable cars hushing by at thirty, shots from the practice range, the clicking brake release of golf carts, their ascending whir.

There I sat, often into the afternoon, while Jean lay at home on the couch. Dying. Dying *right now*: part of my mind could never quite reconcile itself to this fact. Sometimes, too, I imagined her sitting at the library desk, reading. Periodically, over the past weeks, I'd ventured downstairs to check her progress. Page 36; page 59; page 72. What miserable hours those must have been for her, wading through that dismal history, its registry of property owners and public works. By now I'd begun to suspect that we had not come down here for her, that all this time she had been working to renew not her own past but my future. I tried driving her around, looking for certain oaks or hollows she'd known as a girl, but we never found anything. There was nothing left here for her to recognize. Perhaps the place even frightened her, in its strangeness. Yet she continued to feign nostalgia for my benefit: even the look in her eyes as we first crossed that bridge, how she clasped our arms—even that had been a gift. Once again, everything had been about me. Once again, I'd gotten it wrong.

Such were my thoughts at the brink of that piercing blue pool. The humidity nauseated me; I'd sit there all afternoon, my chest filled with a coldness despite the heat—Jean thinking I was out golfing. This was what awaited me. This, my life after Jean. Birds, boats, Buicks. This plashing pool, this idiotic lullaby. Whatever you leave behind when you come to a place like this, you had best leave utterly, and not look back as it sinks out of sight. You golf, damn it. You swim.

Standing at the edge of the pool one afternoon, shirt still on, I found myself leaning forward, thinking: I'll take brains in the gutter, thank you.

> *Dale Duster Bridge was built in 1923 and named after the North Carolina cotton farmer who lobbied it into existence. Erected at the site where eighteen years before there had been a river fjord, the bridge would rejuvenate local farmers by cutting thirty-five miles from their interstate commute. When the bridge finally opened to traffic in April, several thousand turned out along the banks for barbecue and speeches. The ceremony concluded with two young men from Charlotte, J. P. Miller and Red Powell Jr., flying a Curtiss biplane beneath the bridge. "The trucks of the plane kicked up a thin mist as they touched the surface," reported one of the many spectators lined above.*

The Foresters invited us over to watch the Fourth of July fireworks from their dock. Jean hadn't left the bedroom all day and said she didn't feel like going. But later I found her dicing up a fruit salad in the kitchen, and we all walked over. Zach and I carried a cooler between us. His hair was by now sun-browned and summer-shaggy.

Around back! read a paper plate tacked to the Foresters' front door. We followed a white-pebbled path around the house and worked our way haltingly down the steep backyard, ice sloshing from the cooler. Barb hollered up greetings from the dock below, bounding fitly up the railroad-tie steps to help Jean with the salad. Jean told her not to be silly, it was just a salad.

The dock sagged under our weight as we filed on, one corner dipping under. There were too many of us. The Foresters had set out some plastic deck chairs, and as we sat we took care not to knock one another over. The dock jounced under us as the girls ran up and down the soggy pier waving sparklers and keeping a shy, lovesick distance from Zach.

Ted took the burgers off the grill, and we worked to balance the paper plates on our knees as we talked. Soon Barb caught Jean up in a lengthy discussion of her salad. Ted, Zach, and I watched boats gather around the bridge, their anchor lights coming on in the dusk. I felt good sitting there with my son, sipping beers out on the strange edge of our lives. An odd warmth filled me, and it hit me that soon there would be just me and him. I think Zach felt this, too. This was the first time we'd all been out of the house together. Whenever I handed him a beer he said, "All right, Winston." I drank more than usual.

By dusk the lake had become a floating city of gridlocked boats. The murkily brilliant sprawl reminded me of our hillside view of Scranton. The flotilla spread almost to the shore, and four or five warmly lit boats floated within speaking distance of the dock.

"Some yahoo killed out there every Fourth," Barb said, already heady with wine. "All come down here from Charlotte"—she swept an arm out at the nearby boats—"so we can't even take our own boat out." Their boat, tarped over, nudged urgently against the dock every time rollers came through.

The Days Down Here

Ted was talking to Zach and me about the newly widened bridge and tax dollars, though I didn't believe he thought very often about either. He said the place just wasn't what it used to be. I got up to relieve my beer-full bladder, and as I tried to weave through the plastic chairs, I lurched to the side, felt a sear across my thigh. "Fuck!" I said, watching the grill tip into the lake. The Forester girls screamed as cinders shot wildly across the water. The grill coughed out a loud boiling hiss and quickly sank. I stared at the confusion of smoke that lingered across the surface. I'd had too much beer, and even as laughter exploded behind me I felt my face crumple and spew tears in a sort of ecstasy of pity. In the dusk, thankfully, no one could see this. "Watch out, Winston!" Zach yelled, doubled over. Ted appeared beside me and gave a congratulatory slap on the back, pointing at the water. I hurried up to the bathroom.

I'd returned and eased into my flimsy chair amid a lull in the conversation when, out of nowhere, Jean said, "Oh—Ham got a job!" Everyone looked at me, then cheered and laughed and toasted me. I explained how I'd been hired to teach shop at a high school over in Clover. I would start in the fall.

Everyone glanced at the water, where the grill had gone in. Again, hilarity overtook us.

I raised my beer and said, "To the fallen digits of Clover High!" Everyone realized I was drunk, I think, and laughed at me with quiet affection. Zach leaned over and gave me a jostling, one-armed embrace.

It was dark then, and as we waited for the show our talk fell to murmurs. I felt full from the burgers and beer, but warm, loved, and incredibly peaceful. Then I glanced over and saw my wife. With some alarm I realized she shouldn't have been kept out this late. In the course of the evening her laugh had become a sort of silent, undulant leer, barely discernible by the lake lights that caught her wet teeth and eyes. She was *sick*, I suddenly realized. She shouldn't have been out. I had to get her home. I had to get her back immediately, I decided.

"Jean," I called, pushing up from my chair.

And just as she turned to me, the lake welled with a wide cheer under the pink pulse of the first explosion.

• • •

Those summer days grow harder and harder to recall. It's February; everything has been over for six months now, and the days are pulling me into someone I don't recognize, like it or not.

Yesterday I was wrestling the drawer in and again summoned forth that cigarette. When I saw it I sat back down. The winter light outside was bluing toward evening; frost encroached across the window wells. I found myself taking the butt in the tips of my thumb and index.

I wondered which, between this desk and me, will outlast the other.

I continued turning backward through the history, reversing my wife's progress, setting each page faceup on my right, revealing each time on my left the blank back of another. I couldn't help running my fingertips over the blankness, feeling those ridges of script. What was it I hoped to conjure from those ripples?

I put the cigarette to my lips. I breathed in the singed hollowness of its tip.

February.

• • •

I have learned that sometimes there is a final "rally" before the end. Days before dying, hours even, people get out of bed and stand bolt upright. They open curtains and get dressed for church, yell out for five hamburgers. They whiz out of the driveway on a squeaky-braked bike.

By August Jean was no longer having good days. The pain kept her in bed mostly, and even the act of my sitting her up against some pillows was enough to take her breath away and make her queasy and dizzy. A Charlotte doctor gave her drugs to keep the pain under control, but nothing like what they'd give her in hospice when finally we took her, just days before the summer unraveled.

A week before that move, two weeks before the end, I returned from another spurious golf outing at the pool and found her standing in the kitchen wearing a sundress and large straw hat I'd never seen.

"It was up on the closet shelf," she said, following my gaze. "Jumped right on me."

I asked what was she doing, whether she was okay, and if that was a bathing suit she had on under.

"I feel like a swim," she said. "I feel like a swim in the lake." A shadow, something like that of a bird, seemed to flicker faintly over her eyes.

And so it was that we decided to take up the Foresters on the long-standing offer to use their boat, docked behind their house, keys in the ignition. I went to the bedroom and pulled the golf trousers off from over my swim trunks and stuffed a duffel with towels and sunblock. Back in the kitchen, Jean stood at the counter making bologna sandwiches. She iced them down, along with three beers, in a small cooler. The straw hat had a remarkably cheery effect.

Across the street, we practically tiptoed through the Foresters' yard, sidestepping pansies and buttercups, avoiding the gaze of windows. Walking down the sagging pier, I sensed that behind me Jean was looking down at the old beach, at the mussels in the shallow, tea-colored water.

I pulled the moldy tarp from the inboard-outboard Bayliner and left it bundled on the dock. Oxidation chalked the hull, and the interior's beige and navy vinyl was speckled black with mildew.

It was a Saturday, and the channel shook with dozens of buzzing boats and jet skis. I climbed in the boat and held out my arms, but she waved me off. The sharp-pitched rollers discouraged skiing and made Jean's climb into the boat, with her weakened legs, visibly difficult. A hundred yards out, four or five boats had moored together; a radio's station identification laser-gunned across the water.

Jean pulled herself into the passenger seat, gathering the tote and cooler beside her, a bit out of breath but smiling. When I turned the key, the engine chugged weakly to life. Finally, together, we could slip out onto the rollers.

As I idled into the channel, Jean, in the back-facing seat, must have watched the shore, the houses, the whole peninsula get smaller, flatter, more indistinct. Soon we were rocking precariously, boats squalling by and sloshing wakes over the gunwales, and it became clear I'd have to speed up and get on top of the water. I had never driven a boat before. I eased the throttle all the way down.

We rollicked wildly up the channel, chattering over wakes, crashing through rollers, stung by unexpected whips of water, both of us crouched over in our seats, feet wide-planted, holding to the windshield. A plastic cup swirled up from the floor, floated for a moment between us, and flew away; then my Winston Racing hat was gone—I looked back in time to see it hovering over our white contrails. When I started to

The Days Down Here

loop back, Jean leaned over and grabbed the wheel, shaking her head. Her own hat too was gone. We couldn't hear a thing but the hilarious rage of that boat.

We were out of control, but Jean never told me to slow down. It seemed we were past that.

I searched endlessly for some quiet lagoon, but down every cove we veered toward there paraded a succession of skiers, tubers, and obstinately puttering pontoons. I continued farther and farther up the lake, still at full throttle, bones aching from the vibration. Up by the dam, we finally discovered one cove that was mostly empty, save a few bass boats drifting in shadow along the shore. The water smoother there, I let off the throttle, and the shock of silence washed in with our own bloated wake, which mounted toward the stern as if to swamp us.

It was a short cove, and we idled all the way to the end, curving out of sight from the channel, and finally found our lovers' lagoon. I cut the engine.

"We're lost now, Ham," she said, weakly lifting off her sundress.

"It seems. I think we're near the dam."

"Well. It's sure nice to be away."

"It is nice," I said, unsure of precisely what she meant.

We crawled up into the open bow and lay there with our feet up on the windshield. Messiaen pondered quietly from the radio as water blipped about the hull beneath. A crow throated from the pines. The sun lay over us heavy and raw. It felt good to overheat, to sweat.

Once a year, you may notice, our lake "flips." That is, when the water's top layer becomes colder than the bottom layer, the two instantaneously invert. Overnight the lake's surface turns crimson as bottom mud is lifted to the top;

the colder surface level is subsumed, introducing, inversely, a clarity to the lake's bottom. This phenomenon lasts for two days or three days at most. . . .

After our sandwiches and beer, Jean climbed up on the bow and dove out into the lake. There seem few human gestures that so defy death—or, say, ignore it—as a solid dive, with its pure, piercing action. It is a beauty hardly human.

As she sprang off and arced firmly through the air, the flaccid flesh of her thighs and buttocks shuddered around the explosive hardening of her long leg muscles. Chin to chest, hair startled outward as in some girlhood summer, Jean seemed to achieve an assumption of flight. Fingers pressed, toes tapered: a beauty no longer human. It seemed she could pierce through everything, even death. If there was a splash, I do not remember it.

There was silence—she below the water, I on top.

Then she surfaced. Screaming.

I leaned over and only then deciphered beneath the lake's bronze the cloudy hulks of firs. All around the boat. A Christmas tree dump, likely set up by fishermen. Probably everyone else on the lake knew about it. Some local tradition. Jean scrambled toward the boat, flailing at the surface and trying not to paddle too deeply. But she was caught—a blackened twine had tangled around her ankle and foot. She yelled as though I were not right there, reaching down to her. Behind her a brown fir broke the surface and seemed to sigh. She screamed again. "I'm right here," I called. "I'm right here."

Memory, like history, yields to different layers, and I don't want those final September weeks to be what stays on top, what reflects off the surface. If I look back, that's what's most vivid: the smell of tomatoey vomit that filled our bedroom; the way Jean's underwear hung loose between her legs; how the jaundiced cheeks ruined her smile; the sight of her lying in bed at night under that alkaline-amber streetlamp, body curling and uncurling, mouth opening, knuckles striking the headboard her father made for our wedding and that we'd thought, tying it so carefully into the moving van, would bring us closer to home. She grew strange to us. She began to wander, and one morning I watched Zach walk clothed into the pool we never got around to cleaning, startling her as he took her naked, floating body in his arms and carried her inside the way I'd once seen him carry a quarry worker with a broken leg and lay him down in the back of a pickup truck. That was the day we took her into hospice.

It's those images that are brightest, I'm afraid—those weeks when I forgot about love, about my wife's touch; even forgot what she had looked like as I stared at her gaping, gasping face. Thinking of that is enough to keep me down in this basement forever.

Three weeks after she died, I was wandering the afternoon-lit house one day in October and found myself sitting again before this desk. Neatly folded laundry was stacked on the dryer: she'd been too weak to carry it up—both of our lives sifting and settling, finally, into this basement. I knew before opening the drawer that the history had been completed, that I'd find again one neat stack, the blank back of its final page turned up at me. But it wasn't wholly blank, that final surface. Having slogged through this place, she had tried to begin again with what she had failed to find:

Running   running in from the lake   in through the

Jacob White

screened porch   Feet wet with sand and pine needles
with blood   mussel shell   in through the porch   to
Grandma rocking   running   running

And what more was there to say? What more?

I turned the back page over and began to read. I read backward through the whole history, trying, I guess, to re-trace her footsteps—chasing her, just as she chased whatever it was she was after. Just as our old historian chased what he was after. Beneath our lake, he writes, lies an older lake, and beneath that lake runs a river—the old Catawba, moving still down a furrow along the lake's belly.

Surely this summer isn't the history we wanted. Surely what we'd wanted to live on is the story of how we met at a contra dance forty-five years ago, held in spin by our pinprick pupils, falling in love quickly and fiercely. Or the tale of that icy morning Jean gave birth to Zach. What I want is a history of the contours of her face, her jaw line, of how she smelled, and her dishrag laugh. But I've only *this* history; that other stuff runs beneath it. I've only this one to keep afloat with. Maybe it was the same for this old ghostwriter: I sometimes think of that army-issue machete, of the war he must've fought in. And yet it was this other history he adopted, or that adopted him.

Even as my memory fails, even as I reach out for some-thing of our life, for some darkening murk of memory, I must at the same time seal myself off from it, cauterizing the past beneath this last summer. If I do not stay on top of this lake, I'll drown. I'll drown and there'll be nothing of us left. Per-haps the lake will absorb me and this ultimately unimportant pain—just as it absorbed that wisp of her blood, which for all I know swims out there now somewhere, which for all I know turns the lake red for one day every winter.

The Days Down Here

What slices deeper, finally, than a mussel shell on a child's sole in summer?

I hadn't known about that, by the way. In her occasional and reluctant indulgences of that memory, she never mentioned the blood, the bite of shell in her sole.

"It's all right," I said that day as she lay on the boat's nylon carpet, wrapped in a yellow towel. She wouldn't let me hold her. "It's all right. It's just trees. Just old trees." Again she slapped me away, and I squatted next to her for ten minutes, two fingers on her ankle as she curled into herself and howled.

Then, later—hah!—the boat wouldn't start. The radio must have drained the battery. We sat there waiting for a boat to come by, but there were none. The afternoon was getting late. Finally I went up into the open bow, rocking the boat with my steps, and pulled up several cushions until I found some mooring line. I leaned over the front of the boat and tied one end into the prow's eye hook. Then I tossed a cushion over and dove in after it.

One arm around the cushion, the other holding the rope over my shoulder, I kicked until the looming shape behind me began to turn and move. After I got through the slime-fingered trees, it took me an hour to reach the mouth of the cove in this manner. The sun had got behind the trees. The channel was mostly emptied, a few boats hurrying by on their way home. Eventually one peeled off toward us. I let off stroking and floated on my back, panting and dizzy.

I felt the water thrum as the other boat eased alongside. "Winston?"

The channel had gone glassy, the light a deep orange. After Zach and another kid helped us in, I could do little but

117

crumple to the ski boat's floor, leaning my back carelessly against the knees of teenage boys and girls. The boat was a true inboard, with an engine hatch humped right in the center. I sat in one aisle, Jean in the other, leaning against a pile of life vests behind the captain's chair. Zach drove.

"What about their boat?" Zach said. "We could tow it back."

I waved it off. I was out of breath. "So much for being neighborly," I said.

I could only see the top half of my wife's head over the engine hatch, her brow like the pitch of a meek tent, the eyes black and bitter as pine forest.

Zach looked at the girl next to him. "Time left for a pull?" he asked, grinning, his knuckles glancing her thigh. Clearly he'd known these four kids all summer, which explained the coming home wet, the glorious tan. He stood, letting the girl slide into his chair. He pulled from the bow a long, flat, fiberglass board with rubber boots on it, what I now know to call a wakeboard. He threw it in the water and then picked up the handle of a rope tied to the roll-bar tower above us and threw it, too, into the water. He dove in. He came up and whipped his hair into a bird's beak at the back. In no time he was on top of the water.

He'd spent the summer on the lake, yes. A summer on the lake. Would he eventually try to balance his whole life on the pearl of this summer? Would he discover one day how slippery were these moments of grace?

Imagine my son. Imagine him there on the coppery flats, swinging out next to the boat. The rope slackens, and he seems almost to stop. Then he digs in his heels and leans back as if to sit down—the rope tightens, the tower above us creaks, the boat seems to bog—and he is whipped in, cutting a quick buttery slit toward the wake. His wet hair trails behind him, as do the strings of his cut-off jeans.

My son explodes into the air. He is upside down, his now-long hair sprayed out toward the water; he is gliding over the far wake, over the flat water beyond—lifting, still lifting.

I had no idea. He is marvelous.

The tower creaks more loudly and the boat teeters as, with some sinewy grace, an upside-down Zach pulls himself back around, lats rippling. Caught in this moment, in this knot of time and space, he is utterly strange, strange in the way of true and awesome beauty.

I try to understand the violent grace we are seeing, knowing that I will be unable to remember it. The violence with which one history ends, the beauty with which another begins. Between my wife and me, the engine growls massively through its muffled hatch, deafening both of us. I can see only the top of her head, her hair in a private fury.

He lands—his weight punching the water; the board makes a satisfying tamping sound. A sound that expresses my son's density. The rope slackens, snaps taut again; the boat heaves. Fiberglass crackles around us. I can hear the squeak of his rubber bindings as he carves back toward the wake.

He falls once—smacking hard into the water, ripped from his bindings. The boat circles. "Fine," he faintly yells. "One more."

But it's many more. Well into dusk Jean and I watch him go back and forth behind the boat, mostly floating through the air, upside down, twisting and untwisting in a pendulous, alien language. The girl drives and the other boys watch in a silence that could be boredom, awe, or simply the pleasant swell of indolence. My son's vigor seems misplaced in this twilight. He rides for an hour more, back and forth through the dusk. As he swings out into the flats—in that brief pause before the boat pulls him back toward the wake, that moment where the rope hangs slack and he's just coasting—we can see his legs tremble.

I look again at my wife, beginning to sense the cruelty of our discovering now, only now, such strange beauty in her son, something she won't have time to understand. In October a wakeboard company would fly him to Florida for the winter to train. This spring he will begin touring across the country to compete. He'll be on TV, he says. He'll be on late at night.

Perhaps I, too, should write a history. Something to be dug up by a future homeowner. But I'd hate for my memories to collapse into a sprawl of sad, brittle pages. Sometimes I hope my memories will outlive me; other times I just want to make it through the winter.

We were there, my wife and I, crouched in a stranger's boat one late-August dusk. We leaned shirtless against the warm knees of tanned kids and watched our son. Him holding on to that rope. Finally the day grew dark, and his movements, graceful as they were, became smears of shadow, something we could interpret only by the way the boat bogged each time his heels sank in, by the creaking around us, and by the shock that ran through the hull as he left the water.

The Hour of Revision

Is it all right if I say I wish my son were a little older? That I am sort of waiting it out? Till he can drive, maybe? Then I can tell him not to speed over Buster Boyd Bridge, because on Buster Boyd Bridge they will nail yo ass. That's how I will say it: nail yo ass. They nailed my ass there twice. My daddy got his ass nailed on Franklin Boulevard in Gastonia once and could never give me the keys without saying, "Take it easy on Franklin, because on Franklin they will nail yo ass." Hearing your father imitate a country judge, going so country with that yo that he is almost Creole for a second, is exhilarating. It is exhilarating at that age to have a grown man stand before you in a suit who has had his ass nailed. That comical *yo* he puckers with pained deliberation, as if still smarting from the nail—but so straight-faced you know he's having a little laugh at it. At himself, probably, but a little at you too, or at the idea of you ending up in the same mess as he before you are quite ready, knowing full well that you will end up in the same mess as he before you are quite ready, because that's how it happens: Ready or not, they will nail yo ass. "Easy on Franklin," he'd say, a little wince as he spread the paper. "Nail yo ass." My daddy could really toss it off. Like a judge. Which you'd swear he was,

121

by that lipless escarpment of face, by the pithy black eyes that made the warm sound of nail yo ass so unexpected. I can't recall it without recalling too my first sip of whiskey behind the house one night, Kirby's little trash fire sending into the trees its dim far-flickerings and murk, Kirby the greenskeeper at Daddy's club. What was he doing there, out by the toolshed with me, alone—my god, slipping me whiskey? What was he burning? Had my father contracted him for some yard work? How complicated, these adult negotiations. I handed up the flask, thinking I'd tasted some of Kirby's adult lips on there, and watched flames weave and slip among one another.

When you're a kid and someone says nail yo ass, you can't help but wrestle with the phrase literally. Metaphors don't have their shells yet. The difficulty of setting a nail in a soft cheek of butt bothers you, and you're faintly humiliated by the thought of having it done to you, by the baring of your silly white bottom. What's more, the yo implies it will be some country hand such as Kirby contracted for the job, which he would prosecute both crudely and expertly, no one there to protect you, not even your father. Your father has seen your silly bottom and is a little bit teasing you with the nail yo ass thing. It will be years before you are in on the joke. Though by then the warning will have come to sound idle and heart-less, the little nail yo ass a purely self-satisfying little flick of phrase, something to scatter the million other tired thoughts scuttling around in his mind. Years later still, you'll wonder if it were not some graver irony that had beset him: *In either case, they will nail yo ass.*

I doubt I will feel like a country judge when I say it. I wonder if my father even did. He was closer to a judge than I'll ever be, or anyone these days. Reading a paper now is like a joke. Picture me looking up at my son from my living room's

The Hour of Revision

"workspace," my face palely aglow with a screen of Yahoo spam. Not to mention the mother's father will have already bought him his own turbo hatchback, so he won't be asking me for keys or even to go out because, god forgive me, I live in a condo now, my authority diminished with the square footage, apparently. The workspace is a breakfast bar. "Take it easy on Buster Boyd Bridge," I will say, stooped over the breakfast bar, "because on Buster Boyd Bridge they will nail yo ass."

Or maybe it will be okay. Maybe some of that sweet stupidity of his will hold out and he'll stand there as I did, quietly moved and nodding, as if hearing a low rumble echo behind the clouds.

Or he'll blink at me with those clicking eyelids of his mother. He might even have enough of his mother in him to say, "They nailed your ass because you're an impulsive driver, it's a problem."

But I have years to prepare. I do drills in the foyer mirror Friday afternoons until he bursts in and throws his duffel at the foldout. Halo, O'Doul's, pizza with banana peppers, and the weekend is gone before I can get a handle on him.

You have to say it slow, slow but measured: *They will nail yo ass*. When you hit ass your eyebrows are raised, your mouth deadly serious: They will nail yo ass (!). The warning hangs for a moment on your forward-tipped face, your fine bottom teeth just visible. All severity and humility. For what is more severe, finally, than the humility a father?

Of course, it all hangs on the nail. The nail is the secret to the whole thing. It took me years to realize it but that's where the joke happens, if it even is a joke. My god, shivers the child, a nail! And the father, spreading the paper: If only it were a nail. If only it had been a nail. Yes, it has to be a nail. The simplest thing in the world.

Feather by Feather

He stands in the road, concussed, a typical creature before God or before no one. Behind him some ways a small bridge crosses a creek. Beneath the bridge, a truck. The truck, his, lies on its top. Waving in the clear current there is hair. Hair he isn't sure whose. He is having county issues. What county is this? he wonders. And now wonders if county is an issue at all. Hair, a mossy yellow ghost of it from under the lee side of the truck, contemplating in the shallow current. County *hell*, he says and does not say, though the question sticks with him. He decides to walk.

Walking, he pretends to take in the tree line. He squints at a pretend distance. Then, in the real distance, pinetops tipple; an oily black star of crow switches trees. Now he's pretending *not* to notice the distance.

The real break comes when he can't remember if he talked to his mother on the phone this morning and *catches* himself not remembering, thinking it's something he'd remember. Then he catches himself not knowing if it is morning or getting late. The sun's pinched at that dramatic, unsure angle.

He feels hilariously *large*. Texas football player large. He could have a cowcatcher jaw and be named Macky or Duce.

Feather by Feather

He feels this way and then he doesn't. His hearing gets, like, cold. He can hear air in the trees, air around his wet body, the on-moving of world. And then he's feeling pretty small. He feels hunched and small and knows that's what he is. More Beetle Bailey than Texas lineman. At one place his tongue finds gum instead of tooth. He doesn't feel a lot of character at work.

A bare thigh, solid and warm, just minutes ago in his hand. He slows, looks over his shoulder. Then, a friendly *tick* on his temple: the asphalt has risen to meet him. His lips say something against the warm grit, dumb as slugs. He pushes up with the hop-to of a military drill. But as he rises to a crouch it's like he's got bowling balls around his neck, and he's doing a funny downhill dance over the road shoulder and into a cow-sized ditch. He lies there.

The lake, he remembers. He is supposed to meet her at the lake. A girl. A woman. Not his mother. Or maybe his mother. The ditch cups him coldly. A wire pulls through his mind and he doesn't like it. He clenches his eyelids. He listens to the air.

He hears a lake nearby. A *big* one. An earthy, yawning sound. He thinks about how much he could go for a lake. Your chin on the water and you look down and your legs are moving and orange. Here I go! he once hollered at his mother, then lost himself in a back flip off a dock. Now he's wondering if a lake is something you can hear.

Again, he catches himself.

San Sebastian

Up ahead, a big-boned boy struts down the middle of the street, really strutting, left shoulder dipping eight inches with each step—fast dip, slow correction. Brand new white tee shirt to the back of his knees, the shorts themselves sagged to mid-thigh, his bottom buck-naked under that shirt for all I know. In the great landfill of the ages no one will tell us apart. I don't know where my husband is.

When I overtake him I see he's one of those broad-knuckled boys with more man in him than he knows what to do with. Baseball-sized knots accent the hang of his long ludicrous shirt. I turn and ask about Dawlie.

"Do you ever see a man drive up and down this road in a wrecker? Lives up at the end there? The chainlink yard with the big pecan?" I point behind him.

His head is titled back so he has to look down his face at me. Beads of sweat under his eyes. The eyes dilate and his lips hang apart not unamicably; he is not *pursing* them at me. I am a woman well up in years and can still bring him to attention.

"Well that is my husband. I want to know if you have seen him. He is I believe on foot."

San Sebastian

He leans away and waggles his head over the curb, then hitches his drawers, gearing up for more strut. Then he's off, slow and stiff as a zombie.

Dawlie can't be making much better time, given the sciatica. It wasn't half a minute after the mower shut off I looked out and saw it by the street, empty, yard half cut. I keep waiting for summer to bust his tomato.

Three blocks ahead, two white men approach loosely on bikes. I cross left to their side of the road so I can ask about Dawlie. But then they turn into the forest, disappearing single file into the pines and low fronds, a plastic bag full of tall cans swinging from the handlebars of the latter, who has been pushing along with one foot instead of pedaling. If you see white men on bikes here they are homeless.

Across from the path into the woods, there is a house so full of black children that they stop up the road. The toys alone shut down traffic weekly and this is never corrected. Dawlie is patient and will get out of his wrecker to move the toys one by one to the grass. Meanwhile kids chase each other around the yard in packs, bursting out into the street, or clustering around the crabapple in front to jerk out some boy by the leg. It seems to be an orphanage, if that is the term still, or some illegal daycare situation. It's just a little old brick ranch house. There is some regulation going on here but there is not nearly enough.

You will imagine what people call this place. It is tolerated only barely by the neighboring blacks, who have come up over the years. The blacks have the smartest siding on the street and are laying in bright new driveways. They're generally retired and by the looks prudently so. The scorched lean-tos and blattering flatbeds are gone, replaced by mauve Buicks to match the pale plum carpet inside. They've prepared.

Meanwhile the whites have started to rust out. Our gutters sag, our shingles are going. People need to get on their yards.

When I look back, the boy behind me is gone. I imagine him doing his grandmother's dishes, then sitting on a made bed to suffer through geometry or program a computer.

In the woods I kick through a trail of frozen dinner trays until I reach a clearing that overlooks the marsh and the San Sebastian. Across the river, a little train goes by with toy-colored cars. The men lying around the clearing, six or so, look at me blankly or do not look at me, even though this is private property and I could be the owner here to arrest them. In the middle of the clearing squat three men. Dawlie is one of them. His shirt is open. He's grinning. The two other men are pouring gasoline into the earth.

"Come look at this," Dawlie says. He stands and steps back from the tarry spatter radiating from a small sphincter in the ground, into which the two other men have inserted the spout of a one-gallon gas can.

"They bought that gas from me," Dawlie says. "I come just to carry back the can." He chuckles. "I thought somebody broke down."

"They bought it?"

He tweezes a curl of bills out of his breast pocket like he used to his near-empty Winstons. "Three dollars. That's pump rate."

"Won't it get in the marsh?"

Dawlie nods, laughing silent and hard at his shoes, face red. "Tell her," he chokes out.

No one looks up. The gas can's air hole gasps like a little baby saying *puh-puh-puh.*

A few times a year Dawlie finds one of these men asleep

in the shed and has to warn them about the pigmy rattlers living underneath.

"Come on, now. You got to tell her."

The pourer's helper says, "I don't know, Dawlie." The primary pourer is apparently in the grip of concentration.

"She's all right, man," says some bearded trash splayed on the dirt in direct sun. "Lives back up 'air"—swinging his head up the street. "That's Dawlie's wife."

"You got to tell," Dawlie says, wiping a finger across his eyes.

The pourer's useless helper, wiry with long rotten teeth and Eddie Haskell eyes, rocks back on his heels and explains they aim to fill the earth with oil, ma'am, and sell the land to a prospector. Already, off behind a log, dozens of sticky motor oil bottles and a few three- and five-gallon gasoline containers are piled together with a rope through the handles. "We'll have to haul them out before the speculators get here."

"Haul out your beer cans too?" I say.

"It's got to look like a natural rupture," says the primary pourer without looking up. All I see of him is his blistered bald head and tight wiry glasses. He's got the boxed, trimmed temples of tired math teachers.

"Do oil rupture from the ground like that?" says the pourer's helper, now rocking back on his heels and holding his knees and watching vapor ripple the air around the hole. "Naturally?"

"That ain't what oil looks like when it come out," says a fat pink-eyed man off against a tree, under shade.

"It will look like *something*," the pourer says. He won't look up.

"Y'all two don't know how it works," fat man says, trying to laugh but breathing like he has a condition.

"Son, you talking to a *operator*, now." This nonsense earns laughter from the circle of sun-bleary men and even from the pourer himself.

"Good afternoon," a very old man calls from under a low frond when the laughter abates. He's propped on elbows in the tiger shadow and appears to have just come to. He addresses me in the measured twang of my grandfather. "Do you have cocaine?"

"How deep is that hole?" Dawlie asks the pourer.

The pourer has been staring at the hole since I got here. He pushes the little spectacles up his nose. "It goes on down."

"It's deep!" a terribly drunk young man hollers from a log. He's been trying to sit with his legs crossed, his forearms leaning on the top knee, but he can't make it work.

"There was yellowjackets coming out of it," the pourer finally says. "Popped Sweetwater there four times in the neck. Next day he comes back with that five-gallon tank over there full of gasoline. Pours it all down that hole. No more bees."

"No more bees," says the helper, who I guess is Sweetwater.

"We been pouring for three days now and it ain't near filled," says the pourer.

"One of you boys own this land?" I say.

There's a glance dance. "*We* own it," two or three say together, looking then at the pourer.

"*Y'all* own this? Y'all pay the property taxes? Buy all that oil, too?"

Dawlie looks over. *All right, Sadie, all right.*

"It's ours," says the drunk man on the log. "Who the hell are *you*?"

"That's Dawlie's wife, man," says the bearded man in the dirt, apparently dying. "She lives back 'air."

San Sebastian

"What the lady's telling you is you ain't got papers," shouts one man behind me who has been lying on a wooden pallet with an arm over his eyes. It's the first he's spoken and he's paler than everyone, the youngest by a decade or two. His long black hair is wet and combed and hangs right on the dirt. Under the skinny arm his face is gaunt and gray. He wears a striped polo and denim shorts that look washed. His legs are hairy sticks that taper into bulbous white sneakers. "Ain't somebody just going to give you money for this land without papers, oil or no oil," he says straight up into the air. "You over your head."

"Somebody gonna *want* that oil," says the pourer, his bluster flagging now.

"It's half gasoline. And you there smoking. Like to lift us to the moon."

"He's right," Sweetwater says, flicking his cigarette. "We need more motor oil."

"Motor oil ain't *oil!*"

"It's got oil *in* it! It *looks* like oil."

"It don't look like ground oil!"

"Y'all planned all this high as hell," wheezes the fat man. "It's got too serious."

"Yeah, we *shock-and-awed* them bees, shit . . ."

"Man," says the young one on the pallet, lifting his forearm a few inches off his black eyes so I see for a moment the lipless Panhandle face, "you done ruined the whole ground. I just wanted to come here and sit in the shade and *drink. Damn.*"

"My days drinking outdoors is over," says the pourer. "I got appointments with two potential clients tomorrow, lobby of Flagler Hotel." He pushes himself up and hands the gas can back to Dawlie. "You and yours grab y'all a beer out that bag. We Christian. I got to lie down."

Humanities Club is at two and I won't make it now. "Come on, Dawlie," I say.

"*Come on, Dawlie*," jeers the drunkard on the log but everyone ignores him. Dawlie's peeled off his shirt to swat the bugs and they all see how his slick white back is wider than it is tall. But Dawlie is also most parts deaf and already reaching into the plastic bag.

I know for a fact one of the men here is a rapist. The paper said one was out and living in the woods here—roaming our yards like some neighborhood Labrador. There was a picture, Billy Graham with glasses and a wadded little mouth, and something about a fused knee. But all homeless men around here have a knee that won't bend. The pourer's fine little spectacles recall the rapist or a rapist from a movie, but when he stands and walks briskly to the shade he is too short, his knees fat and limber. "There's some fume coming out of there," he says discreetly to fat man, sitting down next to him.

Dawlie, limping about like one of them, walks over slowly and sits on the log by the drunk that mocked him, gas can between his boot heels like he's ready to go. But he doesn't go. He sits there chuckling with dazed slack eyes as the men around him talk holes in each other's head. I am somehow afraid to leave him here—my presence in the grove has lightly stupefied the men—so I walk down to the marsh and watch hermit crabs skittle.

Two minutes into this reverie, there's a scuffle behind me, then a scuttling in the woods, squeals. When I turn, three of the men are stamping around in the clearing, among them the bearded one who'd been dying in the dirt—"Hell was *that*?" He toes an empty plastic Diet Pepsi bottle next to a dark spot where he lay. "They throwing bottles of water at us."

"No." Fat man is smelling two fingers. His shoulder and the side of his hair are soaked. "No, they not throwing water." Several plastic bottles lie around the clearing.

The Sweetwater one walks in circles, shaking his head and scratching the back of his neck. "They got us, y'all. Admit it, them kids got us good . . ." The man is crazy.

"Where's Tully?" the pourer says. The skinny one on the pallet is gone. A few slats are stained dark.

"Gone after them," the bearded one says.

"The kids?"

"Little head popped up over that bush there. Nailed Tully about point blank."

"Lord."

"Them kids don't want to mess with no flashback," says man on the log. Dawlie sits there next to him, still, smiling and watching, the whole left thigh of his shorts soaked. Another Diet Pepsi bottle lay a few feet away. He's hit worse than any of them.

"Dawlie, look at yourself," I say. "You had enough?"

Dawlie nods. He does this preemptive forward lean that he usually reserves for Thanksgivings, half a minute on the edge of Kaylee's couch before finally rolling up on his legs and out the door. It's the closest he's ever managed to good-bye pleasantries.

But before he can get up, a black woman I've seen a thousand times but never talked to swats through the fronds and stands looking at the oily spatter, then at the men. I feel like she's probably done this before, since neither the men nor she seems surprised to see each other.

"My girl say y'all trying to burn up the woods."

"No," says the pourer, standing and waving his hand tiredly. "She misunderstood."

The woman's eyes run all over the pile of gas and oil cans. "What she misunderstood?"

A few old boys open their mouths to answer this but can't.

"I had just come back here to investigate what they were up to," I say. "My husband Dawlie and I."

The lady ignores me. "Y'all pouring stuff in the ground?"

"We doing some work," says this Sweetwater.

"Y'all doing work," she nods.

"You won't believe this," I say, "but—"

"Y'all aren't setting to burn nothing, are you?"

The pourer quickly stands, hand out, shaking his head. "No, no, no"—*Newww, newww, newwww,* like you say to a small dog hopping at your candy bar. He walks to the center of the clearing. "No, ma'am. This is a work site and frankly ain't safe for kids."

The others like this and nod.

"You putting stuff in the ground there? What y'all doing?" Her eyes finally fall on Dawlie and the gas can between his heels. He doesn't notice. He doesn't even care he's wet. He sits there staring at nothing, mouth shut with that half-attentive grin. He looks odd here in the forest, younger. Awake.

"We trying to bring in some development," the pourer says. He cleans his spectacles in his shirt, shaking his head. "We *trying* to bring a little money to the neighborhood."

"The neighborhood? What neighborhood? I done called the police."

"Your little girl threw pee at us, lady," says the drunk on the log next to Dawlie. "*Pee.*"

The woman gives that electric stink glare that black women can give when they are offended. I am tired of this glare.

134

"Ma'am," I say, stepping forward, "the children did come back here throwing pee. They hit my husband Dawlie—by accident, I'm sure. We live right up the street—"

"They live back 'air," says the bearded man.

She looks at me like I'm a talking tree, then takes a step toward the pourer, thumbing over her shoulder. "And your friend—one come blazing out after them Hope House kids—"

"He's a veteran, ma'am. He's a good boy."

"Well the dog on him now." She shook her head. "Was in my yard creeping."

"The dog?" fat man says. "It attacking him? He getting attacked?" No one stirs.

"Tully been through a lot," says the pourer. "He can't handle no dog."

"Go on get him then," says the woman. "He in the garage with Max. White house, green shutters."

Still no one moves. Fat man yawns. "That dog at bay, then?"

"Long as he don't move."

"How long you going to leave him there?"

The woman looks at Sweetwater. "Till the police come, darlin."

"Lady, we covered with pee," says the pourer.

The woman nods. "Might help cut that oil." And it's only now I get it. She is going easy on them.

"Listen," I say loud to Dawlie, "I got to get to Humanities Club," even though Humanities Club is over and the lady's already turned and swatted her way out of the clearing, without once acknowledging Dawlie and me even though she knows we live right down the street and always have.

"Y'all come on back any time," the pourer says, and Dawlie follows me out of there as the men resume their boardroom gibberish. Walking back up the path, we hear kids racing through the thickets alongside us.

"They pouring gas back there!" one yells from the street.

"They 'bout to burn it up!" the other yells, tearing loose of the brush ahead of us—his sneakers going *pow-pow-pow* on the pavement. Across the street, the other Hope House kids run circles around the house, yelling, "Burn it up! Burn it up!"

We ease back up the street, Dawlie limping and me slowing to his pace. Somehow I'm carrying the gas can. "I feel a little loose today," I say.

"The heat."

"I feel like trash."

He nods. "Paid me pump rate for that gas—you believe that?" He shakes his head.

Up from Hope House is a neat little bungalow with green shutters and a clean white driveway. A German Shepherd sits out in the middle, its snout pointed at the open garage, very erect and still with its triangle ears.

The dog glances over its compact Egyptian shoulder as we pass, face char black, then resumes its observation of the garage. Observation is the only word.

"There's that ole' boy," Dawlie says, and I look. I have to squint, but he's back in there, sitting on a workbench against the back wall. Hands in pockets, big white sneakers dangling and stirring. It looks cool in there.

Dawlie pauses to wave before limping on. "He ain't in too much trouble."

The tide is out and the afternoon has that scooped-out smell. It's turned quiet; the Hope House kids have disappeared inside. A prop tour-plane mows the long afternoon sky. We need to get on our yard.

San Sebastian

There's a loud *whap* from the garage, but when I look back the dog hasn't moved. "That man's going to get hurt, Dawlie."

Dawlie reaches over as we walk; I hand him the empty gas can. He holds it on his other side so it isn't so strong. "A German Shepherd is a smart dog."

Your Father Needs More Time

The Jew

She said have a seat and went into the kitchen, a mirror image of my own down the hall, but then again, because she was seventy-five, in no way a mirror image. The kitchen was of course nothing but a pen created by the breakfast bar, if that is what they are still called, if people are still willing to call them that. People here rely heavily on the breakfast bar. Not for breakfasting or even for drinking at, but for how it holds the room together. Holds everything together. Breakfast bar sums it up.

The old Jew stood in there under a neon, twisting out ice. Her knuckled back was to me and through the dyed frizz her scalp shone. I could see the ball of her skull. "I'm going to give you lots of ice," she shouted. "I see how you go through it."

"The usual ice is fine." We hollered as though from different rooms.

"You eat it. Crunch crunch crunch."

"Okay."

"You macerate it."

Your Father Needs More Time

"It makes no difference to me."

"No difference to him," she said coming around the breakfast bar, like she knew everything, everything. I had just dropped off my second month's rent.

It had been during my first week in the complex, giddy still with the new catastrophe of my life, that I developed the merry habit of knocking on the jamb when I passed her open door. Just a neighbor checking in, twirling my mail key until invited in for a drink—late enough so it wasn't conspicuous I hadn't been at work, but not so late as to be really good-timing it. A prudent little cocktail hour we never ruptured. The window light gave way to lamplight, and I got buzzed on a mild immigrant mother fantasy, she on some sort of low-frequency flirting, or it was the other way around, or it was both ways. I was to leave when her show came on.

"You don't have a dog, do you?" She held out over the coffee table a trembling tumbler thick as an ashtray at its base, where it was tinted a pale blue from some ribbon in the glass the eye couldn't get at. The pebbly wrist was just managing, and as I half stood to relieve her of the heavy tumbler, cupping a hand beneath to catch the icy slosh, she teetered backward, her black eyes holding hard on me as if for balance, or just awaiting an answer. A dog? Before I could respond she shook her head and walked back to her chair. "Everybody here has dogs."

I nodded and instead of talking tugged back the knees of my slacks and rested the drink in my crotch. It was what I always did. My little sham of down-on-heels gentility. Like a country judge who had been disbarred, or debenched, whatever, then bewildered out here for some somber penance. This sham carried in it somehow the sham of the patient son, the autumnal lover.

"Harold and I always had dogs," she said. "I've had fifty dogs. There was a Scottie named Early Chester that sailed out to North Haven with us each summer. For weeks it ran rats out of the scrub brush and dashed down to the rocks and back barking. I don't think you are supposed to let those kinds of dogs run loose. Something killed it."

Harold, was it? We were advancing. We sipped our bourbon and ginger ales. "I don't have a dog," I said.

"I know that. I suppose I meant at your real home."

Just over Buster Boyd Bridge was South Carolina and the house and the woman and boy. I shook my head. "There is no dog there, either."

"Well. Don't get one now."

We drank to that. I picked up a little mahogany rhinoceros, tuskless. The Jew had built around herself crypt of such trinkage, things of tortoise and jade, china and brass. Lacquered Japanese things. Crap, really. Whether she had yachted in Europe or lived out of Northern dumpsters, it hardly mattered, she clearly wasn't from Gastonia. I hoped it was clear I wasn't from Gastonia. I replaced the rhinoceros on the chattering glass table. "I am having company," I announced. She was doubled over, fumbling under the recliner for the remote.

"Well it's good you should," she said, subtle as queen, no way ever to decipher the inflection—whether it bespoke the delicately dismissive patrician authority I had originally suspected and that last month made me feel I'd joined some colony of reposing expats, or was just more of the practiced gibberish that had begun to recur over the weeks, like the silken blouse with its soiled cuffs, revealing beneath its frayed veneer something crepuscular and empty that I was coming to suspect more and more lately and that, upon suspecting, made me feel at times that I was sitting alone in a room with a dressed up cockroach. The show she watched every night was *Hee Haw*.

"I think it probably is good," I said to myself.

"Company," she said. Her sandaled foot had begun to stir and erect itself and bounce as it did before the show came on. She had found the remote and was holding it in her lap. A palsied thumb caressed the red button. I chewed the rest of my ice to snow. I raised the tumbler and turned it in the lamplight. "What would you call this?"

She looked through the murk at me, blinking, the black eyes little pebbles at the bottom of time. "In Jerusalem, I think."

"I mean, this color. This blue."

"Dead Sea."

The Village

Outside, the walkway rumbled with bass. As I neared Dale's open door the walkway's aluminum railing rang with each concussion. My feet vibrated, my fillings.

"Mr. Hawthorne," I said, lingering in the doorway, bass bouncing into me like big rubber wrecking balls. I had smelled the pot from the Jew's.

He danced up from the couch, bandy in his baggy jeans, and turned down the stereo. Here was one of our obsequious Southern drug dealers, mantis-faced, with eyes of the cleanest white, the thinnest blue, piercing and empty. "What up, Cleve?" My name sounded bright and simple in his mouth, like I were made of Nerf. He delivered a swooping handshake.

"Is this the party?" I craned in and gaped around his apartment, a bungling father crashing a kegger. It was my line.

"Yeah dog. Word, word. Yo Cleve, I need you to do something for me."

"You got it, bud." He'd borrowed a drill gun from me last week and returned it the same day, battery charged. *Around here, we borrow something, we bring it back same day*, he'd declared. I was starting to like my little village. "Shoot!"

"That spot they gave you out there in the lot? I need you to use it."

"I take your place again?" I shook my head. "Hell. Lot on my mind, I guess. Lot on my mind."

He lifted his chin and smiled as though I were standing about ten feet back. "It's just, you know, I had to park up at the third phase. Then walk back down."

"Third phase?" The third phase was a quarter-mile off. "Jesus." I pictured a tiny little figure in the distance, working his way down the steep berms that separated each phase. Tiny little baggy jeans. I shrugged. "I guess someone was in my spot."

"That's what the Condo Association's for, Cleve. That happens, you call them up." He made a thumb and pinky phone next to his head.

"Well, now I feel like an ass," I said, glaring hard so he'd feel like an ass. Condo Association? How about a joint, man?

"It's okay, Cleve, but you been here over a month now and I won't mention it again. It's only, I had to park up at the third phase. Then walk back down."

"Loud and clear. Anyway," I smiled, "I'm expecting some company."

"Cool, cool. Just, you know, keep it straight out there." He didn't quite laugh. "We good?"

I stepped out into the hallway and squinted off toward my own door, as though contemplating fairway yardage. Certainly I wasn't going to apologize to this kid, standing before me bare-nippled with the milky tan of a teenager. "You got it," I said and walked off. His door eased shut behind me, the bolt shot a little hard, then the throbbing bass and a little voice inside. "...That's right we good, Jack ..."

The Arborist

It was already dusk as I approached my own door. With a little inner shiver I saw my neighbor's door gaping open, which was rare. I had seen him exactly twice since I'd moved in. He was in his forties and wanted to be left alone. Once in a while I heard the low murmur of a TV. He cleared his throat in his sleep.

I passed the doorway quickly, slipping a glance from the side of my eye. The apartment was dark but for the dull light of the sliding patio door in the back, open, a thin white curtain lifting into the room. The breeze wafted through the apartment and out the doorway, stirring my hair. A silhouette rounded the couch toward the patio door, a shirtless, bulky torso; the neck of an emerald bottle glowed at his side. The curtain filled and rose and spun like a bell to receive him.

Company

A condo in Gastonia is no place to receive your son for the weekend after forgetting his birthday the weekend before. I had prepared a gracious speech but just in the door he wiped off his mother's kiss with a uriney "Jesus!" and I saw I couldn't give an inch.

"Your mother says you been hollering at her."

"She's a hypochondriac."

"Well, go easy. What's wrong with your shorts?" Beneath the aqua corduroy shorts hung a good two inches of plaid boxer.

He made a show of sparing me the withering pits of his eyes. "Dad, this is how Mac McBride and I wear them."

"I see. Well, I'm a little out of the loop lately. Grab a coke." I went back to my bedroom and returned wearing yellow swim trunks over a pair of plaid Bermudas. My son was kneeled in the den setting a CD carefully in the tray of a nasty little NAD stereo system I had and which, along with the fifteen-inch Cerwin Vegas hulking in the corners, I'd soon pawn for alimony. He barely glanced up but there was a satisfying face drain. "Jesus, what a gooner." Only ten and all these Jesuses.

"What are you putting on?"

He frisbee'd the jewel case at my chest so I had to fumble at it like a fogy. "Gigantigrit," I said, turning the thing over. "What is a Gigantigrit?"

But he'd sunk into the couch, his head already stooped with a cool impersonal list, like he might fire up a joint, and I saw the connoisseur had a lesson for me and I should assume a listening attitude, basically shut up. I hung an elbow off the entertainment cabinet and tipped my head and let my eyes coolly disconnect, aping him as he aped someone whose company is at a premium. "Mac McBride give you this?"

"Shhh!"

And in tumbled a tenor drum with some nuts loose, followed by a creaky upright bass, both bungling along like two autistic hobos and occasionally overlaid by toneless slabs of distortion, maybe two chords in all. The reluctant singer, cartoonishly parched, came legging in and out of the junkyard noise with goofy-hinged quatrains, singing much as I imagined a tarantula might.

At the bright sound of my half-sixer tugged across the grating, my son glared into the kitchenette. "Jesus, what are you doing! Just chill out for once!"

Your Father Needs More Time

I shot up my arms, a man condemned to egg shells, and strolled back around the breakfast bar to my listening post at the cabinet—suckling down half a can on the way. "Hell, if you're going to play it, play it." I flicked the volume and the Vegas sawed us in half. He jerked fetal and clamped his skull and seemed to be saying Jesus again. I held to the entertainment cabinet with one arm, nodding placidly to each car-bomb concussion and trying very hard to keep it together. I then exhibited a loose druggie jog, rolling my head back and closing my eyes and saying, "Yeah, man, yeah . . ."

He went for the stereo but I hipped his skinny ass aside. He went for it again and I bumped him again, and then he bumped me and our bumping became the dancing. Or at least for the brief minute we thought we were in a movie about ourselves and before we each got a good image burn of what the other looked like, which no moviegoer wants to see and which bucked us from the thrall into a private, distracted shambling like that of two boys shambling around the bed of some kind of scary group sex, each trying not to look like he is looking for his clothes.

I can't describe the noise. Imagine a four-inch hex bolt jammed into each ear and crackling with voltage and a lot of bright and brutal damage, stroboscopic flaming tints exploding into your eyeballs. I had neighbors, dozens of them, to say nothing of the arborist, who I somehow knew was just sitting over there in the dark taking it, suffering the noise as just another of the periodic cave-ins of the ditch he'd dug himself. The rest were already pounding at my door probably, my indignant Jewess, Dale at the fore, shirtless and deputized. Another bad apple in 1032. I didn't care, I was a little silly with having my son to myself tonight. It hadn't been a hot year at school. He was "displaying." He was thin. He swung the fat volume knob back and forth as fast as he could to simulate an embolism. "Don't do that, you'll blow the"—but he was off, frogging around the room. He stood before a speaker ramming his groin at it, an innocent spaz-out, or not innocent. No cokes, she'd told me. Not under any condition. Not even on the premises. "Don't do that," I hollered, and my son spun and leered at me from his toxic adolescence. I was leaning on the back of the couch, breathing and withstanding, the noise boiling blood against my face and kicking my heart out of sync. I shook my head. We were doing permanent damage and we were doing it in four pairs of shorts.

"When's the next song?" I yelled. He was on his back now, dragging himself in slow circles with his legs—boring into the carpet. "There isn't any next song. It's just the one. It goes the whole way."

"Epic."

"It's desert rock."

"It sure is."

It was Neptune to me, and he didn't much get it either, but we bobbed our heads and bit our bottom lips, let our eyes coolly disconnect—gooners out of the loop or something worse, something blinded and banished and searching for the correction, while thirty miles away Mac McBride sat in his half-million-dollar bedroom never guessing what motley ghouls danced around his name out here in the desert.

Episode Before Putting on Pants

Do you need more time? Were you not given enough time?

Given enough time. That's how you begin all your sentences at thirty-three. Given enough time, you could get your wife out of the slums, hit the freeweights, improve your posture, leash train the dog. Given enough time.

Of course, had you kept things tidier in places you hadn't thought mattered, things would be, given all your time on this earth so far, better.

Given enough time, even a dog learns to malinger.

You were once a rising so-and-so. You were on your way. And, given enough time . . . well! But now it is late and your medal or whatever has not arrived. You have never seen a medal except once across a room, and because you *knew* the guy receiving it, and because you were, it had seemed, slipping past those years allotted for medal earning, you'd convinced yourself it was being lowered around *your* neck, and, convinced of this, began to pant under its weight and finally collapsed, or collapsed so to speak, for even collapsing lies beyond your courage and other people have moved on with life.

Your mother was competent. She said the good movies end facing west. You insisted for a decade on the merit of bad movies that end facing east because, you explained, these are easier to lose yourself in. Then one day you saw a bad movie that ended facing east and understood that it was bad, and that you *were* lost. You saw the year it was made and wanted only to swat away the curtain of credits so that you could see, if you could see far enough, beyond the hilltops and treetops and through all the grainy miles, your mother, alive still, skiing competently across evening butterscotch, her wet hair flicking and unimportant in the wind.

You thought you were Proust. Or would be, given the time. Then you were given the time. Now you're a kind of animal looking down its own snout. Irrigating the past requires stamina. You're burnt out on the future too. Your activity has become a kind of whittling, your whittling a kind of staring. Proust's million little breaths—you're whipped by the very idea of it anymore. But you got to breathe, you can't be just nothing, not like in space. Try being nothing. Give it a little time. You'll wake up each night to the dull knife at your lungs and the lights in your skull going on-off-on-off-on-off.

Where are you all the time? your wife asks, waving a hand over your face. You're not even present. But you are *exactly* present! You are *deep in it!* Your friend was deep in it. For his wife's birthday he gutted their bathroom, then realized the old notch-joint beams were twisted in a way that made it impossible to figure out, given all the time in the world, where to start reframing. You were too "busy" to help, so three summer weeks he sat in there holding his head, boots dangling into the basement, until finally the father-in-law was called out of retirement.

Three hundred miles away, a middling man in jeans lowers tidy toolboxes into the trunk of a Saturn: about to give his time. How does that make you feel?

Episode Before Putting On Pants

Your *hands* are middling, somehow. They remember what you cannot. It is they after all that have been giving the time. It hits you that you have done a lot of manual work and you wish you could remember it so it could stand to your character. Important credentials are being overlooked, competencies—*you* might have gutted a bathroom for your wife, etc. Let it go. If your hands are middling, you've done what you can. Could. You are competent or you are not. The time has been given. Has given *out*. Only you're not prepared to outlive yourself. Given the time, you're not prepared. For the future. Which you still think is in front of you because you are a child. Though all the lessons are over.

You once drew with the hand of a child an outer-space jungle. I am pretty sure you didn't realize then what a thing you had there—a place where use has no use and there are thick green leaves but no sound and when people talk about "puttin food on the table" or "You got to want it" or "given enough time," it's just mouths making melancholy little shapes. Had you wanted to disappear that was the time to do it. Before the debt began to accrue. But even then there was your mother. There was the time she was given and gave. Imagine her looking for you, calling and calling, and finding only the drawing, your name down there in the corner, and a little note beneath: *Keep me in your heart!*

How does that make you feel?

Yardage

A horse saunters up the middle of Hole Four. Atop the broad roan lolls the small figure of a boy, a limp afterthought to the stolid roll of hip and shoulder. It is late on a green summer afternoon, the sky low and mute, the air heavy with the sweet tonic of Bermuda grass.

The boy's father stands in a buffer of shag just off the green, watching the horse climb the steep fairway toward him. He leans on a chipping wedge, hip boxed out in a pastel contrapposto. The rest of the foursome stand behind the man, strung out uncertainly between the green and the two carts, each holding a club near the head. The father waits for the horse to draw up in front of him so that he does not have to raise his voice. "I hope you break your goddamn neck."

Rolled up on the saddle behind the boy like something dead is a yellow and green afghan. Two plastic gallon jugs hang across the rump, the father's expensive half-inch braid-ed mooring line knotted redundantly through the handles. A rucksack cleaves the narrow, slumped shoulders that stir even after the horse has stopped. The boy will not look at the father. He lifts a warm can of Coors from his crotch, sips off the foam, and looks over the men's heads. He is nine.

Yardage

"He's got a drink," one man behind the father says.

"That animal belong up at the summer camp?" says another.

The first man looks over at the second, then back at the horse. "He got that horse by Jesus from Camp Thunderbird. He took it." The two guffaw without actually laughing, their blue eyes bright, mouths slack and disgorged of sense. They won't step any closer.

The third man, decades older than the rest, steps from behind a cart, drops in his putter, and withdraws an iron. He walks past the other two and across the green, stopping behind the father. "Now that thing is divoting the shit out of the fairway, son, you got to get him on off." He fans the iron tersely over the turf like a metal detector, more corrective than angry. "Kenny, I'm going to walk over to Five while y'all finish up."

"Kenny, I believe he *stole* that horse."

"And somebody's beer—"

"And *some*body's *beer*."

The first man bends down next to the cart and sloshes the cooler across the floorboard. "We out, Kenny. See what's in his sack there—"

"We'll pay him." One of them flops a wallet open. The other swats it away and shushes him.

The father says nothing. His eyes are squinted black stars. He won't look up at the boy, whose fine hair frets and sticks across the pale bulb of brow. He blinks beyond the horse, where the fairway drops and disappears into an emerald valley, then climbs steeply toward the staggered terraces of tees. Theirs were the last carts out. The men are hustling to squeeze in nine. Around the horse's hooves, restive patches of Bermuda twitch with evening air.

"Hell, Kenny," says the second man. "Let him rip. It's the

lake on three sides and 49 on the other. Security will get him and he'll catch hell and you can pick him up later at the gate house."

"There you go," says the man's partner.

"Take your birdie."

The horse takes a step closer and cranes around to lip the sod near the father's spikes. He feels a snort up his trouser leg and steps back with a funny high-kneed stumble.

"Where is Betsy?" he blurts. "You were to look after her. She is your dog."

"I hate that dog."

"What about your mother, then?"

The boy looks down. He flops the reins from side to side with one hand. His other hand holds the beer can beneath his chin with a soft-wristed sideways fan of fingers.

The father nods and turns away from the boy and the horse. He squats, holding the wedge mid-shaft to sight his shot.

"Return the horse," he says, his back to the boy—close enough that the horse could kick him in the head. "I'll see you at the house."

Were the father to see his own smallness in the boy's life to come, it would be too much for him. He is seeing it a little now, squatting beneath that horse, and it is a little too much for him. Two days later he will drop dead of a heart attack. The boy has done his work on him, just as the father has done his work on the boy.

The horse is returned, either by the boy or by somebody sent out for it. The day resolves forgetfully. There is likely a talk, though the father has other worries and is on the phone much of the evening. His mother knows nothing of it and puts the boy to bed, stroking his pale temple. She wakes him early for swim practice the next morning. And a day later his father is dead.

For now, the father takes his birdie. Chips it in effortlessly. It is the most effortless thing the boy will ever see: a man in expensive peach pants and pale yellow cotton-polyester golf shirt sticking moist to his back, the tanned forearms knotted at the wrists into an oaky V. The sleeves ripple languidly. And then comes a soft twist of torso, the tap, the ball hopping up stupid and surprised at first, then tracking calmly across the slanted green and gurgling into the cup. *Birdie* will forever mean this.

The boy used to stand next to the hole, lifting the flagpole from its plug and hoisting it as the ball curved toward the cup, shuffling backward so not to interfere; and only now, as the father retrieves the ball, and walks over to pick up the flag-pole—dusk falling all at once, it seems, the yellow flag whips up as if of its own accord—only now does the boy see that the flagpole is supposed to be simply flung onto the green. By some principle this cannot damage the green but walking it without spikes can. He sees from his strange vantage atop the horse how things are done in the world in which he does not factor. And even in the decades that follow, which provide their own vantage, it will be this dusk of the father that circumscribes his days and nights. The horse and the dream it bore are forgotten in time, the blue-eyed ghosts returning to their carts, popping the brakes and whispering through the pines so there is only the vast yardage of Hole Four at dusk, the forest at its edge already dark and chirring as birds turn to bats.

The Plantation

Evenings now, he stands in his front door, sipping whiskey. His son left, then his wife, so now he develops new customs. Taking the glass from his lips, he senses very clearly how his life has changed. There is a sadness in this vigil, but it is not all disagreeable.

Part of him has come apart. Part of him has begun.

He thinks of himself, now, in the thinning penny-flash of evening light, as the father, because only now does he not feel the cloying weight of that occupation. Only as a vestige does he feel his shape as a man. The house has depressurized, breathes through the doorway. Air breaks over his body. *Father*: it is a word. It is a whimsically grown beard. A silken robe he puts on at night, the house all quiet. The way breezes pulse over him as he stands in his doorway evenings, arm raised against the jamb. *I am the Father.*

Alone for the first time in many years, he goes through a period of lightness, of seeming rebirth. The days skitter with strange, bright hues. The house feels weightless behind him, the door jamb like balsam in his hand. He tenses his muscles, making sure he cannot pick the house up. It becomes apparent that this period will pass.

154

The Plantation

He sips only enough whiskey to scare himself.

They left because he was no longer a likeable man. He had
begun to complain, in his collapsing rhetoric, of what everybody wanted from him—when it was all too evident they
wanted nothing. Realizing this frightened him into a quiet
neediness. His wife—this woman for whom he had built a
house—suffered the erosion of years as if waiting for their son
to bring meaning to their life together. But the boy is twenty
now, sleeping on couches in Charleston. A letter arrived this
spring from the liberal arts college down there saying he'd
withdrawn. The father doesn't have his number.

When his wife said, "You could drive down there, Fran,
find him," he'd reply with a stare meant to seem patient, fa-
therly, but which came off as mean and lost.

When the son left, he left his mother and father to each
other. Later, in spring, Fran helped her load the trunk under
a blooming cloud of dogwood, wintry white petals slipping
off their shoulders. Then the boy, Wynn, didn't come home
for summer.

In his ruddy heart he knows he was made for rougher living. At fifty-eight he has the back and the hands of a Viking.
His chest and arms are ruggedly freckled. Slack red curls,
sagging lips, and wide-saddled eyes bear the gentle drape of
generals. Once alone in the house, his physical capacity for
survival announces itself: his muscles arch, he grabs at glasses too hard, swipes at the phone; his body thinks it is being
turned out into the wild.

He tries to stay out of the house.

He spends weekends roving his yard, snatching up weeds,
toiling against night-creeping rot. Growing up next to an
Iowan cornfield, he was reared on the threat of rot as some

are on religion. His wife and son, he thinks, heeded neither—those slack stares they gave him toward the end suggesting there was nothing to be done. He begins to think often of his own father, how they used to troop through the rows of corn, the soot-eyed man sometimes stopping and unfolding his pocketknife to reach up and excise a black, oozing pustule from an ear of corn. He showed the glob to his son with a short, prohibitive grunt before slinging it to the dirt and slapping the blade clean on his thigh.

He weeds, he trims, he mows. He works all weekend, early to rise, early to bed. He has always mowed the enormous yard once a week—the yard is perhaps the sole mark by which his family was known in the neighborhood—but now he also devotedly tends his wife's old flowerbeds. Lantana, verbena, agapanthas—Garden Club champions. He cannot stand the sight of their wilting. He fertilizes, cultivates, weeds—still they do not perk and sing with color as they once did for his wife. It is summer, and the lingering light allows him a couple of hours in the garden each evening after work: he peels black cotton socks from his stale, pasty feet, steps out into the vigorous blades of grass, among which his feet appear cragged and root-like, as if recently unearthed. He fingers the fragile stems awkwardly, but with time he gets better. Some mornings, even, he manages forty-five minutes or so of distraction on the way out to his car—posting a flower here, rolling some pine straw there. He arrives at the office several times a week smelling of salt and loam.

At his desk, Fran brushes and blows from his reports the black soil that peppers from his fingernails. With great lightness he reels through paperwork, nodding his chin gingerly at clients on the phone. On his desk stands a gold-framed picture of his wife at thirty-three, and a larger one of his son, very young, kneeling in an orange T-ball uniform. Occasionally, after several days of arid weather, he thinks about the flowers, and realizing how far the drive home is, he feels anxious.

At night, as he lies waiting for sleep, he feels his heart—slumping through its work, nudging the surrounding flesh, sending faint convulsive twists through the rest of his body. He lies there feeling each tenuous tug and thinks how this is all that keeps him here.

He is fifty-eight, he wants never to die.

•   •   •

He fled the Midwest and the grim tyranny of his aging father. He fled like the wide, outrushing flatland, like a gust. He was seventeen. In the South he found people busy at new settlements: neighborhoods grew right out of the forest. He'd wanted then to escape the dreary cycle of corn, the stalks like evenly measured days allotted down the rows of years; he'd wanted to *start* something, to rip something of his own from the earth. The last thing his father said to him, hollering it off the front porch, was that he was typical.

He picked up a job landscaping the virgin neighborhoods by day, then nights drove over the border into Charlotte where a community college offered business classes. His stature and broad face gave people confidence; they mistook his Midwestern rhetoric for a kind of wisdom, hardy with nut and grain. He bought a suit, became a salesman, then outlet manager, and soon regional vice president of a refrigerator company. He met a woman named Juna, a waitress where he lunched. With her he returned to one of the neighborhoods he'd helped landscape—right on top of a long dormant plantation: he'd cleared pine groves and dismal outbuildings not unlike those that littered his own farm back home, scooped out fallow crop fields, churning up exotic red clay. What he found upon his return, four years later, was a gated lake community of small hills and cozy valleys, fairways and unexpected coves.

Those first years, he grew drunk with faith in himself. He spent a prodigal amount joining the country club. Then came the boy, wearing the corn-blond crown of the quietly chosen; they waited for it to grow out, darken. It did not. Others were drawn to Wynn as a boy, but approached him slowly. The father, too, approached his son slowly, afraid of his own weight and hard edges, afraid of . . . of what? Those days, the boy ran around so easily with others at the pool, the laundry often turning up the faded rags of tee shirts that drifted among neighborhood boys, and the father had known then it couldn't last. He now wonders if that lack of faith showed in his eyes, if that is what drove the boy out into loneliness—to quitting sports by junior high, to hunching into the backseats of their neighborhood's seediest loners, to sleeping on couches.

Years seeped in. He watched the skin under his wife's eyes turn the fragile blue of tepid milk. Her eyes themselves, he noticed after sixteen years, had worn down to the steel— clicking at him, then away from him in the silence of their house. Only over her flowers did her eyes soften, did her mouth open with forgetfulness.

The neighborhood is still easy to get lost in, one enclave dissolving cunningly into the next. Even after twenty years there, wandering a few thousand feet from home gives an astonishing sense of removal. Walk a mile, and one is delivered to another country, some short back street not visited in years, or ever. Visitors cannot decide how large or small the place is. They turn down cul-de-sacs, thinking it a way out.

The Plantation

After packing off his wife, he drove around some. Every night for about a week he drove through the neighborhood, losing himself to streets that ignited shameless nostalgia: Fairway Ridge, where he used to stroll Wynn when he wanted to smoke a cigar; Sandy Cover Circle, where one night he and Juna tiptoed through back yards to reach the lake shore, but kept getting lost; Blackberry Lane, a long, narrow street he knew he'd been down once, but was unable to remember when or why. The streets, it seemed, laid out distant memories to be explored at leisure, as if what was forgotten could be recovered by mere navigation. But after some weeks of this, the elusive streets, even those deep-shadowed back streets, were just streets and reminded him of nothing but themselves.

He tries to stay off the roads. But his house is just as bad. Finally, he removes the curtains, lets daylight bleach the once warm family corners.

The neighborhood still carries the word *Plantation* in its name. The people who live here think of it as such, refer to their home as the Plantation, and this defines home for them like nothing else can.

•   •   •

He develops new customs.

His wife never grew vegetables. Tomatoes, cucumbers, an herb garden alongside the house—the endeavors of an amateur with soil. He begins to eat the things he grows. He is surprised by the succulence, by the freshness of what he creates. The brisk tomatoes taste like a life he could've had, might still. He plants five apple trees along the front edge of his yard.

He continues to play lightly over the Garden Club flowers—society garlic, butterfly bush, salvias, scabiosa—but grows impatient with their coy fragility, their fading yellows, their determination to wilt. He loves his hardier crops, their fatness, their soil-busting drive to eruct. They make a mess of the garden. It's like having boys roughhousing out front all the time. His hands get sore, blister.

The garden grows that summer into something tropical and out of control. Elephant ears explode from one corner of his house, the front porch shored up by clumps of swollen tomato and cucumber, peppers, even some small apple and orange trees, lemons, things that bend their stalks with obscene tumescence. Several neighbors suggest, rather shortly, he take a plot in the common gardens by the park. The common gardens occupy a swath of power line clear-cut. "You can play Farmer Joe all day long there," Jack Haber chuckles, with no help from his wife. The retirees halt before his house on their daily walks. Some appear on his front porch, ask what is he doing—*What is this trash?* the wives' flaccid arms gesture. The neighbors are bolder now that his family has left him; he is surprised to find himself being bolder back. Briskly he sees the old men and women off his porch. Confused, they walk back up his driveway, leaning on each other, averting their gaze from the sprawling flops of watermelon.

"Staying busy," is his usual reply to these neighbors now. When they stop coming around, he begins going entire weekends without speaking. Monday mornings at work, his voice comes out hard and stale, and he recoils from it. He takes to not talking at all outside work, except to dribble a few comforting words over what flowers remain. The verbena are gone, the lantana too. More flowers pale and die. Then he tears open the ground where they stood.

His adulthood impulses of prudence—the need for groceries, management of bills—surprise him. These remind him he is a father, a manager of life projects. He has kept his scruples.

One Saturday, shopping, he runs into Ron Chiswell and his son Terry in the breakfast aisle. "Where in hell you been hiding, Fran?" Ron says, though everyone knows. Even Terry, a childhood friend of Wynn's, tactfully scans cereal boxes. "Don't tell me you've been playing over at that Quail Hollow course. We got no one to beat up on us out there, Fran." Fran can't help but chuckle. He misses the way friends hollered his name over the heads at cocktail parties, a name suggestive of some somber strength, as if, were he not careful, he would rip the seams of his suit. Now, when his secretary or the teller speaks his name, he feels only an impulse to slump his shoulders.

The coffee shelf's thick aroma works on them. They chat. Ron glances back at his son, then down at the wreck of tuna cans spilled across the bottom of Fran's cart. "What say you to dinner, next Friday? Sue's been wanting to have you."

They were just golf buddies, really. All his friends were just golf buddies.

"Oh, I don't know," Fran says, chuckling.

The summer hits a hot, dry flare before a fall wind seeps in one morning. He watches the delicate petals he has tended all summer bear up for a few days against the stiff chill. He is anxious at work. As they begin to die, he feels alone for the first time, and is touched with a self-pity that drives him to tears one night standing in his doorway, the dark falling faster than he has become accustomed.

He lets off the whiskey, scared at how he weeps for no one but himself.

But once the flowerbeds are cleared, he feels shed of something, some final sinew of rot, as if the flowers themselves had been strangling weeds. He begins to winterize his vegetable garden, and these plants bow out of their season with dignity, making in their roots, stems, and seeds their own shrewd plans for survival.

Winter, he rolls in and out of bed. Some nights he forgets to adjust the thermostat and sees the ghosts of his own breath rising from his bed. The holidays come and with them two calls from his wife, the first to ask of word from Wynn (none), the second to work out which Christmas parties she'll attend. He says he will be a humbug this year; he tries to say this with levity.

Several times, after driving home through Christmas-lit yards, he tries calling the number his wife gave him to reach his son—a roommate's cell phone. But each time, the first half-ring stumbles against a haphazard beep, then nothing. He doesn't know if he is supposed to talk after the beep. He doesn't know if he is out of time.

His own boyhood winters were hard, lonely stretches of life. He remembers once when, very young, he asked his father for a cob of corn. His father grabbed him by the arm, jerked him from the table and out into the wind-driven snow, pulled him out to the middle of a wide empty field. "You see any corn? You see any for miles?" Fran was in his long underwear—they both were. He went to cry, but as he did, the thin skin over the bridge his nose, tightened by freezing wind, split—he heard it. He sucked in a breath, and his father stared down at him, seeing what he would do.

In this way, winter keeps him from weeping again.

•　　•　　•

Then, one morning in late March, he steps off his porch and walks into the yard. The grass has begun to green in some places. A chill morning wind blows; brisk ripples course up his chamois shirt like a rain-fat river. Like something arrived from a great distance, something long in the coming.

He does not go to work. Instead, he drives south into Rock Hill. He returns in a rented truck, pulling a trailer with a small tractor and furrow.

The tractor is loud. It rips open the morning like some chortling herald of spring. He begins in front of his house, tearing red swaths across the lawn, the sod peeling back in flaps. Throughout the morning he plows up rows until he is running alongside the street.

He plows up the garden, even. He decides to uproot the chest-high apple trees, too, just as the leaves are beginning to bud. He drags the compost of his first fruits across the up-churned mud.

As he pulls the furrow across his once pristine lawn, ripping loose large tatters, his yard disgorging great wakes of clay, he feels the sad thrill his son must have felt wheeling up the fairway Bermuda in his car. Security caught his son doing this twice. Both times he had been alone, searching for who knows what in the night.

He plants the corn by hand.

●   ●   ●

Summer bursts open like a soft fruit. His feet grow coarse from walking the rows. Toenails become discolored, gnarled. Calluses blacken. His hands become the hands of his father. When he comes in at dusk, he can feel the coating of salt on the back of his neck. His burning muscles cool into knots.

Upstairs he undresses, steps into the steamed white tile of his shower, and lets hot water soften him. Later, fingering his clean, dried beard, he cannot help but imagine the silken tassels of ripening corn. The appearance of these tassels meant something to him as a boy. He can lie on the couch and think of this in the dark.

He almost never drinks whiskey now.

He sleeps heavily. While he sleeps, the corn grows.

He retires, a year earlier than he is supposed to, without ceremony. Cleaning out his desk, he packs up the two pictures—terribly dated pictures, it only now occurs to him.

At home, he occupies himself entirely with his crop. Sometimes, in the middle of the night, the phone gives off a single ring, and by the time he wakes, he cannot decide whether he's dreamed the sound.

The woman at his door has been his neighbor for twenty years since he's lived here. Her small-featured face, with its pale lashes and brows, has made her local presence easy to forget. Her jaundiced hair is cropped like a boy's, pricked with sweat. She holds a trowel in one hand and is mildly out of breath. "It's just that," she says, making only the scantest effort to blunt her forthrightness, "sir, I *am* a member of the Property Owners' Association, a neighbor to boot, and I have to say, I can't abide"—she sweeps her arm back at the ragged field of fledgling stalks, not looking. The *sir* is a carryover from when she used to visit, giving him a cold eye at the door as she asked to drop off a pie for Juna. With a heavy half smile and exaggerated butler's sweep, he'd usher her and the pie into the kitchen. He never spoke to her.

She regards him now as if she expects as much. Her face is moist from her own yard work. "I just cannot abide—"

"I cannot abide this standing around, ma'am." He offers up the old half smile, swirls his tumbler. He too makes only

The Plantation

the scantest effort. He won't play along with her salty neighbor act, despite the many evenings she sat for Wynn, the matronly support she gave his wife when things got hard; despite the respect he once had for the utter privacy she maintained throughout all of this—never could he fathom how she busied or reposed herself in that flat, dark brown, pine-shrouded house. She stammers on his porch. Her face is sweaty and flushed.

"What are you doing?" She eyes him.

This is the woman who will watch him grow old.

"Staying busy." Her face glistens as he tips back his glass.

The old man taught him to harvest sweet corn when the ears are full and blunt at the tip; the husks should be in a green, tightly folded fist—*Put your hand round that, feel.* He taught the boy how to grow a sharp thumb nail so to pierce the end kernel: it should squirt forth milky white sap; neither dry dough nor a watery gruel—the *too-late tears.* He taught that peak freshness for sweet corn is measured in minutes, not hours or days.

The silk should be drying to brown on the end.

There are signs.

By mid June, the corn has grown to his chest. A few neighborhood cats wander into the cornstalks to die. He finds them mornings—not curled up, as he would have imagined. He puts them under the ground.

One evening, he looks down a row and sees a young boy. Crouched, the boy has his finger out, gingerly touching the snout of one of the cats. Despite an impulse to run the boy off, Fran has the presence of mind to ask, in a mild voice, if the cat was his. The boy stands, looks down the corridor. He gives a look made bold by grief. Fran remembers what lonely lessons a boy can stumble upon in these strange stalks, lessons that stiffen the heart against that first winter. He nods imperceptibly, about to speak again. But with half a stride, the boy disappears back into the corn.

This is the first person he's spoken to in two weeks. The father buried this cat as well.

Even as he returns to these earthy lessons of stone and bone, he has never felt safer. Prostrate, surrounded by the lima-green stalks, he studies the travel of a caterpillar. He does not think about his corn, the threat this caterpillar poses; he thinks instead how wonderfully lost this creature is in its own kingdom.

There was a security he missed and felt he might be finding again in the stewardship of this crop. He whiffs among the fledgling stalks the sweet, drowsy comfort of those first summers here: afternoons stretched out endlessly by the waver of boats echoing in off the lake, by the sound of a distant tee off, a car hushing by at thirty. The boy's skateboard ticking and tacking up the drive, then coasting smoothly away down the street—off to his friends.

The caterpillar crawls over his knuckles.

There were customs then. When Wynn was much younger, he and Fran pranced across the hot asphalt parking lot by the club pool and drove home through the plantation barefoot and shirtless, not wearing seatbelts, eyes hazed from chlorine, the two adrift in the sea of summer. The boy began to recognize certain songs on the radio, sweet, bubblegum ballads, and would demand the volume turned up, not yet afraid to share with the father, not yet understanding that the tunings of the hearts might not be the same.

After high school, Wynn's few remaining neighborhood

The Plantation

friends went to Charleston, and it was another year before Wynn could get in to college there. Of course there was no recovering that missed freshman year; his friends had long branched off into complex social circles, nearly forgetting the Plantation. The boy is still out there, trying to make his rounds—trying, for all the father knows, to recover those old friends. Perhaps he is happy to sleep on their couches. Perhaps he, too, has found some safety. The father doesn't know if his messages, left every month or so—"Wynn, it's your father"—are ever heard.

At harvest, he will snap off the ears with the quick downward push of his father—*a twist and a yank, boy*. He will harvest the field alone, by hand. He has arranged for a local cropper to come by and haul the corn off. He will have to do the same for the stalks once he's cleared them. He will not eat the corn. Corn is not his favorite thing to eat.

•   •   •

Someone has been coming into his field at night and tearing down a few stalks. He finds them one morning, folded to the ground in a little clearing, flattened into a pile as if stomped on. The damage is modest—some bitter impulse of an old neighbor, he supposes—but it disheartens him nevertheless. He begins to understand his father's hate for the trespasser. He drives to the feed & seed with rigid stillness, mouth pressed, exhaling so hard at stoplights he feels it against his button-down.

In the dark, one deep night, he grapples for the phone. He is still mostly asleep. "Yes." The security guard says his son is up at the front gate. The Plantation sticker on the boy's car is expired, he says. "Hello?" the guard says after a moment. "Yes. Yes, let him through."

Jacob White

He turns on the front porch light. He sits on his couch and looks out into the night. The amber porch light touches the now head-high wall of stalks in his yard. They shuffle slightly; appear, almost, to be reflecting fire.

For an hour he sits staring out at them. He dozes.

In his dream, he is cutting smut from stalks in the middle of the night. The black boils multiply before him, he cannot move fast enough. He is on his knees. Then he notices the boils are moving: holding up his blade, he sees a caterpillar moving across the moon gleam. He can see its colors, and in his dream this caterpillar is a memory, the deep green and gold, slow-pulsing inch of some passage. There are more of these coursing up the stalks all around him. They climb out of the dark at his feet, inch toward the moon-wet leaves.

The living room's morning light eases him awake. He squints out at the empty driveway. On his way back to his bedroom, he taps open Wynn's door, but does not slow his pace to remark upon the un-slept-in bed. He has much to do this morning.

That afternoon his neighbor hips through the holly bushes and hands him a pea-green Tupperware container heavy with a hunk of casserole. Then she holds out a white envelope. "Another doozie from the P. O. A. I said I'd save the postage." He stuffs the envelope in his shirt pocket, nods—the old half-smile. She stands there for a moment, hands on her hips, taking in the sight of his tall cornstalks. She laughs, says, "You have lost it, bucko," then turns and walks off.

Inside, he opens the envelope. It's a third notice from the P. O. A. If he does not demolish his cornfield, it states, people will arrive to do it for him. The half-unfolded letter floats into the trash. He feels entitled, having helped shape the earth on which these people live. *Entitled*—a word he would've never used before; the farmer's shield of pride.

He stands before his field and feels how this place was once a plantation. With a certainty he's never felt capable of, he knows corn was once grown in this very spot.

He often tells himself that he has not *returned* to growing corn. That he is not typical, that he has broken into something new and essential. Yet some evenings, while he is so deep in his field he has lost his bearings, a lingering, errant gust will huff unexpectedly across the tasseled ears, making a wheeze akin to his father's rare laugh.

· · ·

He does not mean to step back when he sees the boy. He feels the stalks against his back; leaves tickle his ear. Wynn walks up from the driveway.

The boy's bottom lip is pierced, his hair greasy on top, the rest of him a ragged mess. The slick yellow remnants of what seems a mohawk hang over the pale, stubbled sides of his head—he looks diseased.

"Christ, look at you." The father breathes heavily from a day's work.

"Look at yourself," Wynn says, looking not at his bearded father but at the corn.

He walks in front, parting leaves and stooping his head. Wynn follows. A queer half-light closes in around them. "I'm at a friend's," Wynn says. "I can't stay."

"You see this?" Fran says. They step into the small clearing of flattened stalks. "The old-timers around here, heh"—he crosses his arms—"I think they turned on me, son." He chuckles, glances over. "Son," he says, "I tried calling."

169

Wynn exhales sharply, something like a laugh. "Old-timers," he says, toeing a soiled wisp of pink cotton. He, too, has his arms crossed. "Old-timers, huh," he says, and eyes him for a cold moment. The father sees his own cheekbones trying to wrack the face; the lank boy's shoulders are broadening. The sooty eyes. It's been a year.

"A year," the father says, reaching with his thick fingers to part the blond licks from his son's forehead. Wynn flinches back some, but only some. His forehead is hot, the hair dank. He seems, for a moment, to lean into the heavy palm. The father forgets his kernel-piercing thumbnail, accidentally pricks the boy's temple.

Wynn swats him away—"The *hell*."

The father tries to laugh, reaches to wipe the bead of blood with his sleeve. His son shoves him, the thin arms like a colt's kick to his chest. The father ignores this petulance and again steps forward—"Oh, come on now"—raising his sleeve toward the forehead.

Wynn swings at him.

Chapped knuckles graze his lip, whiffle the air before his face—a kind of awkward, mistimed kiss. It's a halfhearted blow. Startled, Fran stumbles back. His heel catches something; his eyes try to hold to the boy as he falls. There is the sound of his own body crashing backward through the stalks. They crack and shiver, bend gradually beneath him, letting him down slowly enough that by the time he is set upon the ground his anger, too, has lost its heart.

It comes down to this: to gardening in old age, sipping whiskey in doorways, coveting a few acres; to being pinned between a father and a son. It comes down to these tired clichés—the only real custom. Alone, he is the father, a vestige, a parched scroll of no particular interest handed down among generations of men. Alas, the metaphor is not lost on him: he is the chaff, not the thing itself. The estranged son, the gardening, his beard even—all the mark of a wide failure among fathers. Maybe a necessary failure.

Wynn stands in the middle of the clearing. Fran can't look at him, gazes skyward instead. He feels foolish lying there, licking his lip, panting—foolish for not realizing that it was exactly this his son came here to do. Surely he'd meant to hit him harder.

Then he hears Wynn walking off, slamming his shoulders through the stalks, mumbling warbled curses. Fran knows there are no more friends, no one to stay with here. He'd heard no car drive up. He doesn't know how far his son has had to walk.

"Old-timers," his son repeats. He stops for a moment, calls back through the stalks, "Man, kids come to your corn to fuck. No one cares about your—your *crop.*" Fran hears his boy swat his way out of the corn, sneakers squeaking up the drive. "It's just some place to lie down."

Lying upon the stalks, he imagines generations of boys and girls sneaking into his yard by night to make love. He imagines a young boy bowing down the stems, quietly, until there is a soft crackle. The boy's deliberateness as he sets about making a pallet. Shirts drop softly as shadows. How he lowers her out of the moonlight.

Every couple of months or so, he and his wife got dressed up. At the club, he cracked wise and his wife rolled her eyes and laughed, mock-bemoaning him. She wore glossy crimson lipstick that awoke her eyes with appetite. Back home, he kept up the randy act, palming her hip and dancing her up the stairs from behind, dancing some jig: how could he have known, back in Iowa, such a life awaited? How hidden they'd felt in the liquid curves and hills and coves of this place.

She would laugh delicately, emptily, wriggle him off. By this he was to understand that the act was over.

Mornings, he often woke to the eclipsing of light from their bathroom, the door coming to with the snick, it seemed, of his parting eyelids. Then he'd hear the heavy pipes of water let loose, her gold band clinking to the tiles. The exultant quavering of the shower door as it was opened. Then another snick—and his eyelids again shut.

He often felt he was missing the point.

He opens his eyes, now to a clean night sky—a sky viewed through the man-sized hole his fall made in the corn. The sky is crisp with the coming autumn, glitters with a careless scatter of stars. All these stars, they will all fail other planets one day. He tries to remember his and Juna's first night here, the smell of grass as they slept on this lawn in a tent, airing out their newly painted walls. He tries to imagine where his son might be. He will go looking for him tonight, he decides. He will walk to the houses of friends he remembers. He doesn't care who he wakes.

But first he lies there a while longer, listening for the shiver of stalk, the whisper of leaves, for the tentative step of new lovers.

You Will Miss Me

You take me and Reg. Once we hit the lake, weren't nothing like us. We were three hundred pounds each and drag-raced boats down Lake Wylie, which was illegal yet totally unstoppable.

We were always racing. Our mothers will tell you we came hard into this world, that our feet hit the dirt like little hill-backed boars. Juggernoggins our daddies called us for our big heads. We built go-carts. We tore Clover up in those things. Burned across fields like dirt-dobbers, just our heads visible over the highgrass (our heads even then too juggish for helmets). Later it was four-wheelers. Reg suped his up fast enough to hydroplane across his daddy's catfish pond. You have to try and see this: Reg, a good two-seventy by tenth grade, skeetering over that pond. We were both of us what Coach Simpkin called a hoss—part horse, part boss. We blocked but could out-sprint anyone on the team, our thighs massive and hard. We shook the field. We tried out for track but put divots in the asphalt. Nights, whenever we came back to Reg's farm, hollering-drunk after a game, we'd go tearing at that catfish pond, ripping off our clothes as we ran—fast enough, we were sure, to just run right over it.

Jacob White

We weren't brothers but should've been. Only real difference was Reg's fire-red hair, which everyone but me spotted right off as the tendrils of tragedy. His boat said *Reg* in flaming orange letters. Mine said *Hicks* in yellow, the *H* made of lightening bolts. Our rooster tails stretched two hundred yards.

Some talk of us still—those few whose cabins haven't been buried under cul-de-sacs and fairways. Mostly they recall the night Reg ushered in a new era by blowing up Buster Boyd Bridge in his race boat. They argue about what unholy speed he attained on that midnight glass, whether he was borne more upon air than water. Sometimes my name bobs up, too, with stories of Reg and Hicks and the old days. But the stories putter out, and folks just stare off, mostly. They're thinking of the dark red glow of the channel that night Reg burned—the glow you see when you close your eyes. They must know I'm not dead yet.

Living on the lake was our dream since high school. When we didn't have summer football practice, we slalom skied and tubed behind Penny Cocker's boat for whole days. Penny was a few years older and had her own lake house. We'd fly down the lake full throttle as the sun set, her crow-black hair whipping at our faces, and back at Penny's cabin all topple into a golden heap of drunkenness which was part muscle burn, part motion sick, part sun poison, and part Miller Genuine. It was a powerful lake. One night Penny bowed me over the inboard engine hatch of her Ski Nautique. Stars fell across my body in tingly dust, and I whimpered a pledge of love.

At graduation we ran across the stage like gorillas, then took jobs at the Duke Power plant. But one day at work Reg bent over to laugh at this joke I told, and one of his three-hundred-plus pounds shifted in such a way as to split the seat of his safety jumper, which caused us to stop laughing. Talk of possible exposure won him an early retirement. Duke Power was fixing to develop the whole goddamn lake, they didn't need vapors of nuclear sloppiness. After what deal he got, Reg said I ought as well retire too. He could easily have bought one of those houses in River Heights, this gated place up by the bridge. But Reg said how there you couldn't spit out your window without hitting another house or else get fined for it. He decided instead to get a cabin farther up the lake, way back in Little Allison Creek, where it seemed we were pretty much on our own. One whole side of that cove was Tree Geese Landing, and it was all ours.

When we first moved out to the lake, we spent every day running hard, laughing and hollering. We chased deer through our forest, or waded out into the slime-bellied cove and corralled hog-sized catfish onto clay spits and wrestled them. We ran two-inch mooring line across the cove and played tug-of-war. Bored of that, we hung rope swings that sent us through the air like Tarzan. Every Saturday Penny canoed over from across the lake and we'd grill out. Reg bought this old houseboat, and after we ate we three puttered down the lake on top of it till we got to the River Rat.

Even then, campaigns of progress were afoot. As we neared the bridge, we spotted great swaths of red clay in the pineland, some already littered with prefab house framing. We shook our heads, drained beer cans, and Reg or me would stand and stare down this progress as we pissed off the top of the houseboat, something of our regalness eroded.

The Rat was uphill from a gas dock, its orange light snug harbor to a great woodwork of fishermen and lake-prowling lowlifes, some of which knew us from our football days. You saw how everyone got excited when we ran through the door growling, me picking up one of the skinny old fellas and running around the bar with him over my shoulder. We talked loud and knew what to say to make everyone in there tumble to the floor with laughing. They'd drunkenly sack our legs, and Reg and me'd slog around the barroom, dragging all of them. Night fell and we slumped at a table, and it was never long after Penny disappeared unalone down to the houseboat that Reg's eyes flickered dim and he mustered grunts about the end of the lake, how one day there'd be no love left, no woods neither. Back then no one knew what he meant. The others would start in teasing us about who was faster, and Reg lifted his head and we two argued heartily for their benefit before thundering down the pier, ripping off our clothes—Reg banging down the side of the houseboat as he ran past and crashed into the water. We raced the whole three miles home.

Summers got us buck wild but the lake could calm us: just the sight of it some mornings set us to gentler kinds of sabbath. On these days we felt ourselves growing old together and were embarrassed. When fish weren't biting we devoted ourselves to rotgut. We'd sit on our dock and just roast, cicadas sizzling round the cove. We looked off separate directions down the lake and let our talk take wider circles. "No love left in these hills," said Reg, looking up the cove to where, by the mouth, a new strip of houses was going up. "None, seems," said myself, looking the other way, down to where the cove piddled to a muddy end and halfheartedly eroded at a shelf of pine forest. Empties clattered to the dock. We wanted too big, we agreed after a while. Then we squared off on that dock like sumo wrestlers. Whoever got wet had to make dinner.

Summers passed, and we never got tired. Our bodies just started glowing by the end of each day, our eyes fuzzy and sweet-stinging. We found ourselves ravenous, and after steaks or pulled pork, we lay in front of the big-screen till sleep played over us like kittens. Not that crushing sleep of the weary: no, our sleep came as a kind of lightness—the very lightness we'd run or swum all day to achieve. This, what I mean by we never got tired.

Winters couldn't stop us either. Mornings our naked bodies shattered through the icy water, and we raced up the cove and across the channel and back, sidling up midway to box each other in the ear where it hurt most, firing each other up. Some days we took the Bronco out to visit nearby farms. We helped some of the older men fix tractors and reframe barns, and took home cleanly wrapped flanks of beef and venison, which we needed because our bellies were house-fires of hunger.

Then the racing boats. Reg just drove up one day with them on the trailer—I'd heard him honking half a mile out. I cracked a beer and walked out to the porch, where I waited to see his Bronco come dusting down our long gravel drive. Our driveway was two miles long! And there he came: fishtailing down the last stretch, trailering two drag boats, ramped one upon the other, their forked bows raised like missiles.

He'd picked them up at a boat show, both retired from the circuit. The hulls needed some patching, and in both bilges the engine hoses hung loose—doubtlessly ripped out by the high-flying flurries of catastrophe one sees readily on ESPN. I just stood there, saying real quiet, "Mercy, Reg." It wasn't the first time Reg'd initiated me into some terrifying new level of living, but, shit, a look at these things and you knew they weren't for amateurs.

We hoisted them onto heavy-beamed horses in the garage. That night we turned up the stereo Reg bought so loud I swear to god you would see shock waves blur across the cove below, and we each sat in a boat, cold sixers in our laps, yelling over Steve Miller about faraway matters like TV football and girls seen down at the River Rat, while secretly pretending we were racing.

It was a long fall and winter getting those water rockets rebuilt, but we did it ourselves. We amassed a library of tattered and grease-smudged manuals on high-performance boat engines. By March Reg had his cranked; took me till late April. When the day came to slide them in the water, Penny stood on the dock and humored a sense of ceremony by not laughing once.

When we set them in, water came all the way up to the gunwales and we were sure they'd sink. They beveled right into the surface, smooth chips of white. The boats clearly weren't meant for men of our dimensions: I almost sunk mine trying to scrabble at the cockpit. Reg slipped off his and fell laughing into the water. Penny set down her margarita, plucked two bottles of Miller from the cooler, and smashed them across our bows.

Snug in the cockpit, I pressed the ignition, and with a thump that fat engine woke right to growling. Its heaviness throbbed through the boat, fiberglass rattling around me. I smelled that white-gold lightening-test fuel and tried to still my hands on the little steering wheel. My legs splayed below water level, I had to force myself to breathe.

You hit one-ninety on the water, you're born into something new. Every few days we'd explode from our cove: rounding into the channel we'd discern through our blurred windshields a vague geese-like panic as pleasure crafts fled for the shallows. To feel such a mass as our own flung into this kind of velocity made us insane. We'd look over and both be screaming, our gold chains flapping high up on our necks. The boats just never stopped accelerating. We blew all thresholds of wind and logic and would've left our earth's curvature altogether were it not for Hank's Hot-dog Boat, anchored at a sandbar amid a crowd of other boats, and at which Reg and me were obliged to pit-stop and, to fine applause, eat ten chilidogs each before racing the leg back.

As we headed back up the channel, a police boat shaped like a miniature tug would angle into our path, blue lights going, but then putter helplessly out of the way as we blew by, rebel-yelling, exhausts spewing flames of unburned nitromethane, the police boat lost in a white tsunami. At Buster Boyd we would see as always the work trucks crossing over in an endless procession of dust and rumble from North Carolina, and Reg would peel off and run alongside that bridge a few times until he'd thoroughly blasted all those trucks with his rooster tail.

Reg would catch up to me, and that last mile was the most furious. When you're going that fast, no matter if you got your blood brother pushing along next to you, you are all alone. Ripples bite at the hull, and scared as you are, it becomes easier to go faster than slow down.

But the lake could slow us down when we needed. Those evenings the water went flat and buttery, Penny picked us up in the old Ski Nautique, asked us to give her a pull like when we were kids. We'd head up the lake and stop inside a cove as she squeaked this wetsuit up over her naked brown body. She dove in, and we threw out an old yellow kneeboard and a ski rope. Once me or Reg got her going, she spun around on the kneeboard so she was on her butt with her knees drawn and her toes together at the tip. With one hand she gave the up thumb—*faster*—and that's when whichever of us was driving dropped the throttle all the way. We heard the four barrels open, and the wake flattened into a hard, spiny ridge. Water exploded around Penny as she set her heels in. Her eyes closed, her teeth clenched. The kneeboard clattered under her thighs as her weight lifted, and then it was gone, and Penny rose, opening her eyes, flying barefoot across the water. You would love her too.

Out on our dock one day, Reg wondered if the lake wasn't getting tired. For years we'd watched neighborhoods leap-frog up the lake. All around Little Allison Creek now, Duke Power was thinning out shoreline forest for surveys, giving our neck of the lake a sick, wintry look. "Nuclear exposure," Reg joked (he'd been healthy as an ox since his own exposure: we crossed our fingers). Some old-timers who fished our cove hollered how Duke Power was buying up family acreage along Youngblood Road. A new golf community was going in two coves up, one that aimed to make that River Heights down the lake look like a trailer court. The old-timers thought it fair to tell us, too, how they'd seen boys with surveying gear walking through Tree Geese Landing. They were quiet before asking had we signed.

Reg and me looked at each other and our lives began to take shape. I saw his eyes sharpen with the cold pull of purpose. What fire in us this put out, Reg would make up for, beginning with that row of house frames that picketed the mouth of our cove. I was only half surprised the night I woke to find the whole cove glowing red. A police cruiser or two crept down our drive, but they didn't press too hard, knowing full well they'd soon lose this jurisdiction to rent-a-cops. We got some neighborly mail encouraging us to keep at it.

You Will Miss Me

But it was all Reg. There'd be these quiet mornings where I wouldn't hear him in the house—and neither of us went unheard in that house, between the clinking free weights, groaning floor planks, or just us breathing heavily. He'd stay in his room for hours. One morning, finally, he walked into the kitchen, pinching the ridge between his eyes and holding a paper slashed by the same scrawl our fifth-grade teacher Ms. Spurriur had refused to accept as the product of hours of concentration. At the top was written: *Our Homeland: You Will Miss It When It's Gone.*

Penny typed and Xeroxed the page, then stuffed mailboxes all up and down Youngblood Road. She canoed down the coves and creeks, drifting up to bass boats and holding out the flyer without even scaring the fish.

Another night I saw Reg try to slink out the kitchen door in a suit and tie, which I hadn't seen him in since Homecoming. He'd cut his hair (we'd both gone wild-haired and bearded) back how we used to wear it in high school, bristle-short. I muted the big-screen and stood from the couch, licking barbeque from my fingers. "What's up, cupcake?" Town meeting, he said—a euphemism for the vigilante-like crowd he'd rustled into the old chapel up on the McKinney farm. I listened to him drive off to three or four of these meetings before I got the nerve to follow. He never once invited me. In the McKinney pasture pickups and four-wheelers crowded around the little old chapel, which looked fine all lit up. I waited for everyone to mosey inside and shut the doors, then lurked by a window.

I saw Reg grab hold of the pulpit and lay his voice across those people with the soft heaviness of a husband's arm in sleep. Penny stood behind, tending charts and maps. He had come there tonight, he said, to talk of the heart. He spoke poetically of red clay and serried pines. He talked to these people of things he never shared with me, his eyes a cold, sharp blue. The old wavy-glassed panes made it look like he was under water, or I was, one.

One day when it was choppy out, my boat lifted skyward, then flipped back so that I was for a great long while flying upside down and backwards. This was not unpleasant. All I remember is hearing Reg yell his rebel yell from his boat, like a man delivered.

Two coves up, Regal Cay had its grand opening. Prospective buyers gathered at the new marina, and a raised air horn scattered them into a shotgun bidding tour of homes. All 158 lots sold in one afternoon. But the first heavy rain caused the sewage tanks to overflow into the lake, which we smelled from our cove, but which no one farther down toward the bridge learned about until parents began finding little brown leeches under children's bathing suits and called DHEC, who in turn issued an advisory against swimming in the lake for a three-year period.

From the lake, Regal Cay looked a treeless compound of blinding white stucco. Since their marina opened, nearby coves had been abuzz with young skiers and retirees cocktailing under bimini tops. Sometimes the kids found their way into Little Allison, and at least once a weekend Reg and I had to wade out and push them off the mud—send them back safe to their moms and dads. We didn't mind. It was the jet skiers we could not abide, little wasps. We made a potato cannon with PVC, but both felt awful when from a hundred and fifty yards I hit this teenage girl in the ankle, surely breaking it, and she sped off crying.

You Will Miss Me

One night I woke to a gut-ripping clatter echoing in from the lake, my mind half-remembering the shrill whine that led up to it—or maybe just remembering the whines one hears all night living by the water. I knew right off what it was.

Reg was in the garage before me, grabbing life vests and spotlights. He eased the houseboat from the cove as I stood at the bow sweeping the million candle watt slow across the water. Just outside the cove, we heard the voices. My light found a white cutty-cabin cruiser nosed into the water, five or six kids gathered at the stern. One girl bloody-faced and yelling how her nose was broke. This guy kept saying, "Dude!" In the water around them I saw the crumpled shreds of an aluminum hull—all that was left of the small fishing boat. Floating in front of me was half of an old man's head. Those old-timers, ones fished our cove.

Maybe I set a few fires, drove a bulldozer or two into the water. It was a good cause. But mostly it was Reg's cause. I went out with him on some of these weekly missions—hoisting sixers, snickering and flushed like we were going cow-tipping. But Reg forsook the rotgut on these nights, and my part in the operation mostly involved being silent and soft-footed. Other days we ran wild like always. We tore up the channel in our boats at least twice a week—though I was more careful ever since my boat swept me into the sky like an angel. Reg, though, spent a lot of time suping his up, and he had it so hot that each time I had to just watch his rooster tail disappear down the lake like a comet.

I was chasing a rabbit one evening, wet still from being thrown from the dock, when I saw three men in our woods: one suit and two guys in jumpers with a tripod. "You hold off"—this suit, he pulls out a gun. "We know about you . . ."—

he shook the pistol at me. I looked past him as my rabbit disappeared over a ridge. I said, "Mister . . ." I lost my train of thought a second. I did not do what I should have—tenderize those three against a tree, then haul them down to the bank to gurgle. No, I just said, "Mister, y'all killing us." I half-spread my arms, then turned and walked back up the cove. Back at the cabin I told Reg dinner outran us tonight. As if to shoulder some of my defeat, Reg nodded, then walked out to the garage freezer. We'd have to thaw something out.

No one was crossing the bridge at that hour, but some bass fishermen told how two fireballs of debris shot out the other side, skipping down the channel in long dying arcs for a good quarter mile. All this just before a twenty-foot section of bridge dropped.

The explosion woke everybody on the lake—everybody, it seemed, but me. The wood struts and pilings that had been encased in the bridge's concrete burned for hours, the channel glowing a deep, grim red for miles in each direction.

Reg was credited with effectively severing the Carolinas for the year it took to demolish and rebuild Buster Boyd. Duke Power's construction slowed near to a halt, because there wasn't much getting around that lake short of having to drive through four counties. But they found a way. They never found Reg. He'd filled the boat with glycerin.

Then Penny disappeared. I found this hickory wreath on the dock morning after Reg turned to flame. I was alone.

I tried disappearing myself. Where I live now has a name that means nothing to you, or to me, and that is better. I'm sick, too. You don't want to know what I got. It wasn't that red-headed dummy who got exposed. Ha-ha. Man, I feel old. It's true, you may not hear it when I fall—I may sink without

a plunk, without a ripple. But when ones like us leave the
world, there is a shudder, and if you haven't felt it yet, you
will. I think things will be different as you know it, and I
think everyone will be pretty much on their own. But I guess
all this is to remind you. Hicks ain't dead yet.

It's good advice not to live in the past, but be the one
to walk up to me and say that. Those Saturdays Penny came
over and we went to the River Rat, those days were the best.
We got everyone in there laughing, and they wrestled us like
we were giants. One night we were awful tight and asked
Penny why she never took us down to the houseboat. When
she stood and walked out, Reg and me looked at each other
and followed. We found Penny standing on the top deck of
our boat. She ordered us to swim her and that houseboat
back up the lake, which we did, all three miles. Reg and
me swam right next to each other, harnessed to twenty-foot
ropes, sometimes bumping. Behind us the boat creaked and
groaned. Penny laughing from the top deck. Laughing at how
hard we swam—like it was a race either of us could ever win.

Acknowledgements

"Being Dead in South Carolina": *Third Coast*

"My Father at the Mountainside": *Phoebe*

"Bethel": *The Sewanee Review* (as "Night Miles")

"The Oldest City": *Passages North*

"Unvanquished by the Dusk": *Meridian*

"Maintenance": *BULL: Men's Fiction*

"Wolf Among Wolves": *Blueline*

"Out With Father": *Quick Fiction*

"The Days Down Here": *The Georgia Review*

"The Hour of Revision": *New South*

"San Sebastian": *Salt Hill*

"Your Father Needs More Time": *The Literary Review*

"Episode Before Putting on Pants": *Passages North*

"Yardage": *New Orleans Review*

"The Plantation": *The Greensboro Review*

"Feather by Feather": *Quick Fiction*

"You Will Miss Me": *New Letters*

The Author

Photo courtesy of Kevin Dossinger

A South Carolina native, Jacob White studied creative writing at Binghamton University and the University of Houston, where he received the Donald Barthelme Memorial Fellowship in Fiction. His fiction has appeared in many journals, including *The Georgia Review*, *New Letters*, *Salt Hill*, and *The Sewanee Review*, from which he received the Andrew Lytle Prize. He has been an assistant professor of writing and literature at Johnson State College, and continues to co-edit *Green Mountains Review*. He currently lives in Ithaca, N.Y.

About the Type

This book was set in Bembo®, a typeface based on the types of one of the most famous printers of the Renaissance, Aldus Manutius. In 1496 Manutius used a new weight of a roman face, formed by Francesco Griffo da Bologna, to print the short piece *De Aetna*, by Pietro Bembo.

The Monotype Corporation in London used this roman face as the model for a 1929 project of Stanley Morison which resulted in a font called Bembo. Morison made a number of changes to the 15th century forms. Because Manutius did not originally cut an italic for the font, Morrison used that from a sample book written in 1524 by Giovanni Tagliente in Venice. Italic capitals came from the roman forms.

Designed by John Taylor-Convery
Composed at JTC Imagineering, Santa Maria, CA